TWILIGHT ECHOES

A NEW DAWN

JEN TALTY

JUPITER PRESS

"Deadly Secrets is the best of romance and suspense in one hot read!" *NYT Bestselling Author Jennifer Probst*

"A charming setting and a steamy couple heat up the pages in a suspenseful story I couldn't put down!" *NY Times and USA today Bestselling Author Donna Grant*

"Jen Talty's books will grab your attention and pull you into a world of relatable characters, strong personalities, humor, and believable storylines. You'll laugh, you'll cry, and you'll rush to get the next book she releases!" Natalie Ann USA Today Bestselling Author

"I positively loved *In Two Weeks*, and highly recommend it. The writing is wonderful, the story is fantastic, and the characters will keep you coming back for more. I can't wait to get my hands on future installments of the NYS Troopers series." *Long and Short Reviews*

"*In Two Weeks* hooks the reader from page one. This is a fast paced story where the development of the romance grabs you emotionally and the suspense keeps you sitting on the edge of your chair. Great characters, great writing, and a believable plot that can be a warning to all of us." *Desiree Holt, USA Today Bestseller*

"*Dark Water* delivers an engaging portrait of wounded hearts as the memorable characters take you on a healing journey of love. A mysterious death brings danger and intrigue into the drama, while sultry passions brew into a believable plot that melts the reader's heart. Jen Talty pens an entertaining romance that grips the heart as the colorful and dangerous story unfolds into a chilling ending." *Night Owl Reviews*

"This is not the typical love story, nor is it the typical mystery. The characters are well rounded and interesting." *You Gotta Read Reviews*

"*Murder in Paradise Bay* is a fast-paced romantic thriller with plenty of twists and turns to keep you guessing until the end. You won't want to miss this one..." *USA Today bestselling author Janice Maynard*

BOOK DESCRIPTION

A ballerina's nightmare…
A choreographer's curse…
And a deadly spell destined to destroy true love…

Lady Avery Windsor knew she couldn't be the lead ballerina forever, but she never expected her position to be challenged by a legend that would change the fabric of her life. To make matters worse, the new wolf choreographer, Darrell Hughes, brings with him a curse. One that could destroy his pack and flip her and sister's royal destiny upside down.

Darrell Hughes took the job with the local ballet for one reason, and one reason only: to find a way to save his pack from being wiped off the earth by a black magic spell. Avery's father is the only one who can help. The fact that he'd imprinted on Avery years ago, claiming her as his mate, would have to take a back seat. That is until he learns he and his mate are more than fated.

They are the second paring of the Legend of the Fated Moons.

For Jennifer Probst and Mary Leo. Thanks for the laughs!

PROLOGUE

*R*egan Wilcox folded her arms and narrowed her eyes as she watched the little lady brat, Avery, dance with Darrell during a technique seminar and audition for placement not only in the ballet company but classes for the following session. With only one spot left in the advanced junior level, Regan would be damned to see it go to a five-year-old before her. At eleven years old, this was Regan's last chance. She'd be sent to the advanced competition group if she didn't make it this year. The kiss of death for a girl who wanted to be a principal ballerina someday.

Darrell held Avery in a pose, staring into her eyes as if she were the air he breathed.

The water he drank.

He looked at her as if she were the sun rising in the east and he was her sky.

Regan wanted to gag. She was better suited to be Darrell's partner… in dance and in life. He'd made the company when he'd been six, and now, at eleven, many choreographers wanted him to perform in their companies.

Regan narrowed her eyes. The goddamn wolf was imprinting on the royal witch, and there wasn't anything Regan could do to stop it.

The stupid little girl had no idea she'd just been marked and claimed by a wolf. Regan searched her mind for a spell that would destroy Avery and her talent, but Avery's father, the prince, held so much power. Regan was sure he'd know someone had cast a spell and then find out who, which would be one of the worst crimes a witch could commit against another witch. She might be only eleven, but that was the kind of atrocity that would get her powers stripped.

Besides, it was Darrell who chose Avery as his future mate, and he should suffer for his mistake. Avery should end up an old spinster, and her prince father wouldn't ever know what Regan had done.

When the music stopped, the room erupted in applause. The teacher smiled and ran to Avery, hugging her close, kissing her cheek, and cooing about how wonderful she had performed.

"You're something special," the teacher said, cupping her chin. "I know you're going to go far, isn't she, Darrell?"

"Yes, ma'am," Darrell said, smiling, his arm still looped around Avery's tiny little waist. She looked dwarfed next to Darrell.

Regan chomped down on the inside of her mouth, conjuring up the spells from the forbidden Book of Shadows her father kept locked in a safe in his office. He'd lied to the world about its existence and hid it from the eyes of the royal family and council. It was forbidden to keep such a book unregistered. However, her family had always been on the fringe, living under the umbrella of royals and their so-called greatness. Her father resented it but never used his dark magic to do anything about it, and in her eyes, that made him weak. Pathetic. What was the point in having a Book of Shadows if one had no intention of ever unleashing its power?

Her father had no idea she even knew he had it.

But she did and it was high time she yielded the potency of the spells their ancestors worked so hard to perfect.

"Well, well, well," the director waltzed into the

studio, her arms stretched wide. "That was magnificent." She hugged the duo. "Darrell, your career is about to take off like nothing you could have prepared for. And you…" She bent over, cupping Avery's cheeks. "…are going to be the youngest protégée we've ever had in our dance company. I've got big plans for you."

Regan willed the tears forming in her eyes to disappear. All her years of hard work gone in an instant. Half the class eyed her, knowing this had been her last shot. No way would she stay in this room a second longer and watch her dreams fall on the shoulders of a five-year-old.

Regan stormed out of the studio and hid in the bushes by the back door in the rear parking lot, where Darrell waited every day to be picked up by his parents.

It was time he paid for his betrayal.

She knew the spell she needed to use. It would take years for it to take full effect, but it would be well worth it.

Darrell stepped out of the building, glancing over his shoulder and waving to someone.

Probably Avery.

It was now or never.

"Out of the cauldron and into the heart, take this wolf and make the end start. Out of the cauldron and into the flame, take the touch of the wolf's paw and make it maim. With every pump of his blood that is blind, destroy him of his talent and kind. From years of humdrum, his pack will succumb," Regan whispered, waving her hands, pushing the clear puff of smoke at Darrell, watching it slip into his body.

A damp chill settled into her bones. A sharp pain ripped through her joints as she watched Darrell and his family drive off. She hobbled out of the bush, staring at her crumpled, twisted fingers. They looked like her great-grandmother's hands. Old, wrinkly, and mangled. Her toes curled. Her knees twisted.

She sat on the bench. Her limbs became dead weight. Her skin turned saggy and hung like a dress five sizes too big. She blinked, unable to bring the world into focus.

Her older sister and one of the student teachers stepped outside.

"Oh my God. Regan?" Her sister raced to her side. "What have you done!"

"Nothing," Regan said weakly. Her skin heated as if someone had pricked her with hot needles everywhere. She knew black magic had its price, but she hadn't expected it to be so high.

Or so quick.

"Did you use black magic?" her sister asked.

Regan nodded.

"Please tell me you didn't do something to Lady Avery," her sister said.

Regan's tongue was thick, like a brick. She could barely speak, much less move her head, but she managed to give it a slight shake.

"I'm calling Dad," her sister said. "He might be able to reverse the effects of whatever black magic spell you cast."

Regan's heartbeat slowed to a painful pace. "It's too late," she whispered.

1

*D*arrell Hughes sat in the back of the auditorium. A vision of loveliness promenaded across the stage in a pair of nude tights, pink pointe shoes with matching leg warmers, and a white leotard with spaghetti straps crisscrossing in the back. He'd been waiting a lifetime to claim his mate, and Lady Avery Windsor wasn't just any mate.

She'd been visiting him in his dreams for as long as he could remember. Not only was she beautiful with her long light-brown hair, dazzling blue eyes, and legs that reached for the sky. But she had a style and grace. She was poised beyond her years. Whenever she gave an interview—whether it be as a ballerina or as a member of the royal witch family —she did so with a dose of humility that always humbled him.

And she was kind and genuine. Always giving back to the community.

It was difficult for him to believe that the universe had chosen someone of her caliber to be his mate.

He winced as she favored her right knee, doing a basic grand pas de chat. Most people wouldn't notice the slight deflection, but his seasoned eye had seen more than one ballerina a performance away from the end.

Not to mention the ache that twisted in his joints. If he hadn't been dealing with this slow, debilitating pain for the last couple of years, he might believe he was suffering from sympathy pains.

But this was something more.

He'd seen a doctor years before the startling discovery with his pack, and they had no answers. They couldn't see anything wrong with him, but it was one of the many reasons he'd switched from dancer to choreographer.

And, of course, there was the witch doctor.

That had been interesting—and devastating— all in one session.

Tucking his hair behind his ears, he shifted in his seat. He'd imprinted on her when she'd been only five years old. He'd been eleven and her partner for the audition that would change her life. She'd been so much younger than everyone else in her class, but she'd been a natural and all the girls resented her talent, something he understood.

Leaving his mark on her and then having to walk away had been one of the most challenging things he'd ever done. But he'd been a child. He hadn't even come of age. Yet he'd felt the connection to her heart as if they were beating as one. And now, seeing her again, it wouldn't take much for them to mate.

An intense gaze.

A tender embrace.

A passionate kiss.

However, he wanted to find a way to slow down that process. He needed to figure out what was wrong with him and deal with that before she connected to him in a way that bound them together forever.

She did a few turns and a leap.

He was mesmerized by her grace and beauty. Everything about her made him want to jump on that stage and declare his affection.

But that would have to wait.

She had a real knack for picking up the steps with perfect technique and very little correction. He knew back then, as did everyone, that she would be a principal dancer.

He'd landed his first significant role as one of the youngest prodigies in a local ballet shortly after their dance, but he'd left his heart with Avery the day he walked out of the studio.

Yanking his wallet from his back pocket, he pulled out the picture of him and Avery that her technique teacher had taken that fateful year.

He knew Avery would be the love of his life, but he needed her father to save him and his pack from whatever curse or spell had caused his father's sudden death and what would undoubtedly be his demise.

Holding his breath, he blinked a few times. This wasn't the time to fall apart. His family needed him to find the source of the illness that threatened to wipe out every male in his pack.

"Stop the music," he said as he stood and made his way down the aisle, gently placing the image back where it belonged. The cast of dancers came to a slow halt. They exchanged confused glances as they stepped to the side.

All except Avery.

She stood at the center with her hands on her hips and a scowl on her face. A piece of auburn hair fell from her bun. She pursed her lips and blew it to the side. "I'm sorry. May I ask, who are you?" She held a hand over her squinted eyes from the lights shining down in her face.

Talk about a loaded question. "Darrell, the new choreographer," he said, contemplating his next move. The call had come three weeks ago, asking him to take over, and he'd jumped at the chance. He loved being behind the scenes. Not that he didn't love dancing, because he lived for it. Only he preferred to see his visions come to life. There was no bigger rush than to sit back and watch the movement of bodies across the stage while music echoed off the walls, telling a story that broke your heart into a million pieces.

However, he'd taken the job because Avery was the principal ballerina.

The time had come to meet his mate.

And stop the curse, if that was even possible.

"Darrell? As in Darrell Hughes?" one of the dancers asked with such excitement it made his cheeks flush. In all the years he'd been on the stage, he never understood why anyone made a fuss of him.

Whispers erupted from everyone in the background.

He ignored them. "Where's Olivia?"

Avery opened her mouth, but the sound of hard pointe shoes flattened on the stage filled the air.

"I'm right here," a young girl said, skidding to a stop next to Avery. "Oh my God. It's such an honor to meet you." She waved her hand in front of her face and batted her long lashes.

"I want you to try part of this number from the double cabriole to the relevé in fifth," Darrell said.

"Excuse me?" Avery shifted her weight to her stronger leg. "I don't mean to question you right out of the gate. I really don't. But we've only got five more days before we perform live. I need the practice."

"So does your understudy. Just in case." He arched a brow. "And I'd like a minute to talk with you."

"May I ask about what?" She shot her hip to the side, planting her hand firmly on her tiny waist.

Always so polite in front of the other dancers. God, how he wanted to take her into his arms and kiss her senseless.

There was a time and place for everything, and this was not that time or place. Besides, mating could happen anywhere. All she needed to do was accept him and choose to stand with him and they would forever be part of each other. "Places everyone," he said, eyeing her bandaged knee. The right sported a thin layer of tape, as did her ankle. She wouldn't be able to wear those during performances. "Join me in the audience."

"All right." Avery ducked backstage for a second and returned with a towel. As she took the steps into the audience, she dabbed her forehead.

Olivia, an eighteen-year-old with a lot of talent but in desperate need of a bit of maturity and a little more dedication, would soon be taking over as principal dancer. A fact that Avery had to know was inevitable.

Better to leave gracefully versus being pushed out.

He sat ten rows back and watched as Olivia began the piece, impressed by her excitement.

But she was no Avery.

"We were not told we'd have a new choreographer, much less the great Darrell Hughes." Avery settled herself in a seat two over from his, her towel draped over the back of her neck. "What happened to Brandon?"

Darrell had asked the ballet company's board not to tell the dancers about his arrival, which meant no one knew Brandon had cancer—not yet anyway, but that wasn't his story to tell. "He's coming in at the end of rehearsal today to talk to everyone."

"That doesn't sound good," Avery said, glancing between the young ballerina on the stage and him. "And neither does you pulling me from rehearsal. I'm sorry if I'm speaking out of turn, but Olivia does one run-through a day, not random stuff in the middle."

"Things will be done differently with me in charge, and I hope, being principal, you'll help with the transition."

"Is that why you brought me down here?"

He couldn't come right out and tell her she was his fated mate. That would be insanity. A trip down memory lane would be a good start as long as it didn't push her into accepting him as her mate.

He handed her the image of them dancing, wishing he had more than one snapshot. They had performed flawlessly in front of her class. The other students he'd done the same routine with didn't have that special something that she had.

Still had.

"Oh my God," she said, the corners of her mouth turning upward, lighting up the room. "I can't believe you kept that, much less even remember me." She blinked, her thick eyelashes fluttering over her light-cobalt eyes. Tiny specks of fairy dust flickered from her lashes.

She waved her hand as if she were swatting a fly.

He had no idea she was a fairy. He filed that information in the back of his brain.

"You remember our dance?" he asked as his heart swelled with pride. Now that they were adults, the attraction kicked in as if he were a horny teenager. But he was a man, and he could control his animal instincts.

Hc hoped.

"Like it was yesterday." She turned her attention to him. "But I'm surprised you do. I was five years old. I was just a little girl. A baby. And you were already headed off for greatness."

"So were you." He winked. It was impossible for him not to flirt with this vision of beauty.

His mate.

The creature he was destined to be with for all eternity.

If he lived long enough to enjoy the concept.

"I'm stunned." She smiled, staring at the image. "You left the studio shortly after that, but I watched your career as both a dancer and a choreographer. You made me believe I'd be a star."

"I always knew you would be," he said, biting back a smile. He'd never wanted to be in the spotlight, but he was smart enough to know that if he wanted to make it as a choreographer, he needed to spend a few years onstage.

Avery enjoyed the spotlight, so hanging up the pointe shoes would be a major adjustment, but she could do other kinds of performances that would keep her passion for the art stronger than ever.

"Dancing with you that day sealed my fate. I remember feeling like I was floating on air. But you made all the girls look as good."

His breath hitched. Could she possibly know? He didn't see how unless maybe she sensed something, but there was no way she could possibly feel the deep connection he had.

Not yet anyway.

But she will, and he prayed he wouldn't have to break her heart by dying.

More fairy dust flowed from her fingers. She wiggled them, as if to call the stuff back to her body.

He stared at it. Back then, fairies were a mere myth.

Interesting.

"No. You were something special. It was a privilege for me to be paired with you that day." He leaned closer. "It was you who made me look good."

"I thought I loved to dance before that day, but when the music stopped and you left, I knew I was meant to be a ballerina." Her enthusiasm coated the sound of her voice like warm butter melting in all the nooks and crannies of an English muffin.

"I've enjoyed watching your career. You are so incredibly talented," he admitted, stretching his arm over the back of one of the chairs between them, wishing she were closer. "And I do look forward to working with you."

"Why do I sense a *but* coming?" When she handed him the picture back, he took advantage of the opportunity to touch her soft, velvety skin.

The fairy dust circled his wrist and settled into

his pores. It eased the pain in his joints, making him feel young and vibrant again.

He'd yearned for this moment for so many years.

If she sensed it, perhaps she already knew. But he wasn't sure he could take that risk. Not sitting in the audience during rehearsal. He held her hand, fanning his thumb over her soft skin, staring into her orbs of desire.

It was rare that imprinting happened before a wolf came of age. When it did happen, it was usually because it meant something important. Or the universe just knew. Whatever the case, imprinting was only part of the process. She needed to accept him. Which meant she needed to claim him in her own way. From there, mating could either be instant or a dance that took a little time. He wanted time. But that was for selfish reasons.

His pack was dying.

He was dying.

She fanned her hand across her face. It was as if she were trying to hide the fact she was emitting fairy dust.

That was cute.

"I see the bandages, and I noticed you favoring your one leg." He tapped her knee.

"It's nothing more than overuse. I'm simply taking precautions." She rubbed her thigh. "I don't like taking any medications, and I certainly don't use witchcraft to deal with these kinds of ailments. I'll be ready. You can count on me."

"I don't doubt that. Or your ability and talent, but you're not getting any younger." He squeezed her shoulder.

She jerked her head. "Are you suggesting I'm old?"

"No." He chuckled. "But we all know the career span of a principal dancer is short. Have you given any thought to what you're going to do next?" He waved his hand toward the stage as his dancers moved with the music, and her understudy fumbled through the choreography. "You can't do that forever. You may have one or two more years before your age starts to become a factor. Take it from me, going out when you're on top is best. Having a plan is even better."

Avery stared at the stage. Her gaze followed Olivia. "She's good. She has talent. Her technique isn't the worst, but it needs honing. She's certainly eager to please you. But she lacks refinement. She's often sloppy during rehearsal."

"Because she's your understudy." Darrell tapped

Avery's knee. "When was the last time you were in that position?"

"I was sixteen and Gwen was…" Avery's words trailed off.

"Gwen was twenty-six. She was struggling with an injury from the year before and even if she didn't have that bad ankle, she should have retired. You came in after she fell and took her place. Gwen never returned. She felt disgraced and the worst part is she never had a plan for herself moving forward. I don't want to see that happen to you."

"I'm not injured," Avery said softly.

"I didn't say you were. And you're still at the top of your game. You know it. Everyone else on that stage knows it too, including Olivia. Why would she need to prove herself to anyone when she has no chance? She's wondering if her career is over before it started." Darrell arched a brow.

"Are you suggesting I step down simply to give her a shot?"

"Good Lord, no. At least not for the duration of this year's ballet." He lowered his chin. "Have you ever considered being a choreographer?"

"I teach some classes at the old studio," she admitted. "I enjoy working with young students.

And yes, that thought has crossed my mind. But this conversation is a few years too premature."

"It's never too early to start planning for your future." The music faded. He stood, taking her hand. "I'd like for you to spend more time working with Olivia."

"That's not my responsibility. Or my job. Much less my role."

"Maybe not." He tugged her toward the stage. "But this ballet is now under my guidance, and I expect you to put in a few hours with her every day. I want you to help her become a better dancer."

Avery stopped dead in her tracks, turned, and glared. "So she can replace me?"

"No one can replace you, Avery. You've been the principal dancer for this ballet for over seven years. And you will remain so for the rest of this show. If you choose, next year even. But after that, we both know your days are numbered and frankly, so are Olivia's. Every ballerina has to face that fact." He glanced at his watch. "We have one more hour left. I'm going to ask that you take Olivia into the small room and go over the solo parts with her. She's sloppy. And I think if you spend time with her, it will only help you."

"All right." Avery let out a long breath. "I will do as you ask."

"After rehearsal, could you meet me in the choreographer's office? I have something of a personal matter I need to discuss with you."

"Sure." She raced back onstage and looped her arm over Olivia's shoulders.

Darrell smiled. His mate was something special. Now all he had to do was not die.

2

*A*very pulled out her cell and placed it on the vanity in her dressing room. In the three months that had passed since her sister Amanda had first blinked out fairy dust, Avery and the rest of her sisters had all sat around waiting for it to happen.

Only it didn't.

Until today.

And in front of Darrell Hughes of all people.

What the hell did that mean?

It couldn't possibly mean what she thought.

That would be crazy.

Only, Darrell was a wolf. And an alpha wolf to boot.

"Hey, little sister," Amanda said. "How's Twinkle Toes today?"

"That's a loaded question," she mumbled. "How are you feeling? And how's Jackson?" Avery missed her sister so much. Vermont was only four hours away, but still, she used to see Amanda nearly every day. Now it was more like once a month. And it had been three weeks since their last visit.

"I still have a bit of morning sickness, which is more like vomiting fairy dust, if that makes any sense. My fairy powers are growing, but it's hard to separate what are mine and what are the twins. And what's weirder is that I can hear the babies talk. Well, they do not talk, but they have their own language. I sort of understand it. Jackson gets it better than I do. And Dromon and Sadie are always around, yapping at my belly."

Avery laughed. "Sounds amusing."

"It is."

"Well, I've got two weird ones for you," Avery said. "First, guess who is now the choreographer for the ballet?"

"Oh no. They replaced Brandon? You've been working with him for seven years. You love him. What happened?"

Avery took a tissue and dabbed her eyes. "He has cancer. He starts chemo next week. Poor man. But he has a positive attitude and lots of support."

"I'm so sorry, sis. That sucks," Amanda said. "Who did they get to take over?"

"Darrell Hughes."

"Oh my God. You had such a crush on that wolf." Amanda laughed. "Auntie Alley was mortified that you danced with him. She thought for sure he was going to ruin you. She made it weirder when you had all those posters in your bedroom and made Daddy take you to watch him perform."

"Speaking of that crazy witch, did you hear she's still making a stink in prison, accusing Jackson of setting her up and using black magic to do it."

"Yeah. No one is listening," Amanda said. "So, is Darrell still as adorable as ever?"

"Oh, he's something all right. But that brings me to weird thing number two. He's so sexy that I blinked fairy dust right off my lashes. Then it came out of my fingers." Avery waved her hand, half expecting to see the strange particles, but nothing happened.

"What? No way. Are you serious? Have you told anyone? Daddy? Called Trask?"

"I've been a little busy at rehearsal and trying to make sure I can contain that shit so no one notices," Avery said. "But I think Darrell saw it."

"Interesting. It's hard for me to control it all now because a lot of it isn't mine. But what is, I can sense. You'll figure that out. You'll feel something build deep in your core. If you concentrate on that, you can command it to your body. But it gets really hard when the wolf—the mate—that unlocked it is present."

"Darrell can't be that," Avery muttered. "Do you know what that means?"

"Yeah. Either he's already imprinted on you or the fated mating has begun."

"That is so fucking weird. I'm only twenty-four years old. I don't want to be pumping out babies." She shivered. "I planned on dancing for this company for a couple more years. After that, I might turn in the toe shoes and choreograph for a major ballet. Or maybe even start my own touring company. But settling down is not on my radar."

"Maybe not. And who knows how long it will take for that to happen," Amanda said. "But come on, Avery. Would having Darrell as your forever be so bad?"

Avery contemplated that thought for about

three and a half seconds before shoving it to the side. "Not the point."

"I've lived on this farm now for three months. I've learned so much about the myths, legends, and predictions. No one really knows what it all means for the paranormal world. The first pairings unlocked the royal fairies and brought back wolfairies. But even Trask doesn't understand what's happening now. His visions have been scrambled. His word, not mine. And the new history books are at a standstill."

"No, they're not," Jackson's voice boomed across the speaker. "Who are you chatting with, my love?"

"Avery. You're not going to believe what happened," Amanda said.

"Why did you have to go and tell him?" Avery groaned.

"Babe, put it on speaker," Jackson said. "Hi, Avery. Blinking fairy dust, are you? What wolf brought that out?"

"Her new choreographer. But she knew him when she was little. Danced with him even," Amanda cooed. It sounded like she was way too amused, and that annoyed Avery.

"Name?" Jackson asked.

"I doubt you've ever heard of him." Avery sighed as she fiddled with her hair. "But it's Darrell. Darrell Hughes."

"Well, shit," Jackson said. "He's the new pack leader of the Red River Pack. It's a small pack, and the numbers have been dwindling for years. They have only two factions and are one of the topics of the next National Twilight Crossing Council meeting. His father recently passed away, handing the torch to him. Only, it's being treated as an unnatural death."

Avery gasped. How horrible for Darrell. "What does that mean?" She remembered Darrell's father. Actually, she had met his entire family. They were kind and gentle people. And they had always supported Darrell and his dreams. Even if that meant Darrell would defer his role as pack leader.

Or so that's what Avery had read in an entertainment piece about Darrell a few years ago.

"I can't get into the specifics," Jackson said. "That wolf has a lot on his mind. I'm sure if he saw fairy dust coming from you, he's not thinking about what that could all mean for him right now, even if he knows he's imprinted on you."

"You make it sound like that's a given, and that can't be happening." Avery leaned forward, snagging her lip gloss, and puckered. Her heart ached for Darrell. She couldn't imagine losing either of her parents.

"A couple of hours ago, a new history book started. The images are fuzzy and to be fair, Cheryl can't make them out. All that we've seen is a wolf with a bum paw. Whatever is going on with him, though, is getting worse, and whoever his fate is, she's so far off in the distance, we can't see her yet," Jackson said. "Dayton is concerned that she's out of reach because what happened to the wolf has the potential to change the course of our predetermined history."

"I don't want your future to change, but I'm not getting knocked up because of low-hanging double moons. Not at twenty-four."

"If it's written in the stars, it's kind of hard to mess with," Amanda said. "Unless some wicked witch like our aunt casts a spell. So, suck it up, Twinkle Toes. Looks like you're next."

"I'm not listening to this, and don't you dare tell Mom and Dad. I'll deal with that shit." Avery stood and smoothed down the front of her jeans. Her entire life she'd been the sweet little ballerina. Polite and never raised her voice.

Or swore.

At least not in public.

But with her family and few close friends, she could truly be herself. That included dropping the royal act. "I have to go. Darrell wants to see me in his office. I'll talk with you later."

She tossed her purse over her shoulder, sucked in a deep breath, and focused on her core. Auras weren't her superpower as a witch. No. She was a healer and studied potions and mixology in witch school, but much to her parents' dismay, she never fully developed the talent, nor went into medicine. Her dancing took up too much time. But they supported her, and in return, she made sure she carved out an hour every day to continue to hone her craft. But she'd never be a master, and she was okay with that.

And so were her parents. They beamed with pride every time she floated across the stage.

Her auntie Alley, on the other hand, constantly berated her, telling her she'd pissed away her true calling.

Avery disagreed.

With her head held high, she strolled down the hallway toward Darrell's office. For as long as she could remember, Darrell had been the golden child of the studio. The one dancer, of all the dancers, who would be a star. He was destined for greatness, and everyone knew it. Every little girl dreamed of being paired with him when he'd come into the younger classes, even if it was only for eight counts. If you had the privilege of being on his arm, you would look better for it.

But even at the ripe old age of five, Avery understood that dancing with someone like Darrell meant all your flaws would be showcased for the instructors to see. There was no hiding behind his greatness.

Either you stepped out from his shadow and became one with his moments.

Or you fell on your ass.

Avery had not wanted to dance with Darrell that day. She'd been utterly terrified that her name had been called. Not only had she been the youngest in the class, but he towered over her, and she was considered tall for her age with legs that stretched on forever. She thought for sure her dreams of making it into the ballet company would have to wait another year. It wasn't a big deal. She was only a small child.

And the reality was, until the music had started, she had no idea how badly she'd wanted it.

She rounded the corner and tapped on the door. "You wanted to see me."

Lifting his gaze, he smiled. "Come in and close the door." He sat behind an old wooden desk and leaned back in a big leather chair. He pushed aside some papers. His long hair rested over his shoulders. He had deep, dark, soulful eyes that reached right into her heart. He looked so strong and powerful behind that desk. But there was a sense of sadness that filled the room. "How did things go with Olivia?"

"I believe she liked it less than I did." Avery set her purse on the floor and eased her butt into the chair opposite the desk. She'd been in this office many times with Brandon. When she'd first joined the company as an understudy, she had the biggest crush on that man. For a mere human, he was spectacular.

But little did she know he was dating the front office manager, Mike. They made for an adorable couple and over the years, she and Brandon became good friends.

The best.

It broke her heart what that man and his family faced.

She'd have to create a healing potion. It

wouldn't cure. They never did. But it did work with the treatments, and it would ease his suffering.

"Now why do you say that?" Darrell asked. A hint of playfulness sparked in his eyes.

"Because she acted like a brat having to eat her vegetables before she got dessert."

He laughed. "I shouldn't be surprised." He tapped his fingers on a stack of papers. "I'm a little late on reading up on everyone and it turns out her daddy has spoiled her rotten. And still does, buying her everything her little heart demands, but he can't buy her a position as principal dancer."

"No, he can't. And she's really not bad, if she'd put some effort into it. She's lackadaisical and undisciplined. I doubt she practices at all."

Darrell waggled his fingers. "As opposed to the person who practices so hard she's destroying her body? Brandon wrote in his notes that you often come in early and stay late."

She cocked her head. "I'm fine. I know my limits and yes, I push myself hard. But I've had to work my ass off for the respect of everyone on that stage." She held up her hand. "In some ways, people's perceptions of me are no different than Olivia. There are critics out there who are constantly waiting in the wings for the little royal witch ballerina to fuck up. Pardon my language."

"You're not five. I think you're allowed to say fuck if you want to." He waved his hand dismissively as if her choice of foul words didn't offend him.

Well, it offended most people when she used it.

She cleared her throat. "I work so hard because if I don't, people will accuse me of what you just said about her and let's face it. Not only am I a royal, my daddy's wealthy, and I'm his baby. I could play that card if I wanted."

"I'm sorry, Avery, but no one who has followed your career could ever accuse you of that." He rose, stepped around his desk, sat in the chair beside her, and leaned back. "Yeah, sure. Your father is rich. You have the title of Lady. You live a life of privilege. And I get that the interpretation of dance can sometimes be subjective to those who don't know anything about it. But you can't fake technique." He took her hand and placed it over the center of his chest.

And there went the fucking fairy dust. It snaked around his body and if she wasn't mistaken, she could have sworn it giggled like a child racing off to play in the backyard.

She sucked in a deep breath, desperately trying to command it back to her body.

It didn't listen.

Fucking fairy dust.

Fucking wolves.

Fucking Legend of the Fated Moons.

"You also can't fake passion. Two things you have. I know Olivia has the talent. But I don't know if she has the drive or the passion."

"She's passionate in her assumption I'm never leaving and don't want her around."

He dropped her hand, letting his fingers run through the dust. It disappeared into his skin. "What do you have to say about those two things?"

"Every principal dancer needs an understudy. I just wish she took her role more seriously."

He lowered his chin. "How did Gwen treat you?"

"Like a little mosquito she wanted to slap." She shook her head. "Oh no. I see where you're going. I get I threatened Gwen. Olivia is no threat. I'm not saying that because I'm conceited or believe my shit doesn't stink. Everyone is replaceable. I know that. I also do know that my time as principal is limited. I disagree with how long I have left, but let's table that for now. I don't treat Olivia badly. I get frustrated with her because she's on her phone or she pouts. And she certainly never came running for Brandon like she did today for you."

"New meat to impress, but she wasn't prepared, and I can only do so much. Rehearsals can only do so much." He squeezed her knee.

Sparks flew. And not just fairy dust either. Her insides exploded as if cannons were going off in the middle of a battlefield.

"I really want you to work with her and not only on technique. Be a mentor. Teach her everything you know about the numbers. The emotions. I want you to show her that you care, because I know you care about this company."

He had her there. "Can I ask you a question?"

"Of course."

"Did you do this with any of your under-studies?"

"I did, and the first time, I hated it, but if that shifter had his way, he would have pushed me offstage, poisoned me, or sold me to the devil if it meant he got to be the lead male. He didn't care about the other dancers. Or how we all worked together. He only cared about himself. That's the difference between you and almost everyone else on that stage. Brandon picked a great group. But I need to know about Olivia."

"Why?" She folded her arms across her chest and glared. "A few hours ago you said you weren't replacing me. Has something changed?" She blinked. More dust. Seemed when she got angry, it came on thicker.

Good to know.

"No. But it's my job to ensure she's ready to step up if you only need a night off. And she's not even close to being ready. And if she doesn't have what it takes, then I need to bring in someone else next year because, at best, you have only a few years left." He waved his hand through the dust and audibly sighed. "But don't you think we need to talk about this stuff? Because it changes everything."

Her heartbeat lurched to the back of her throat. Her father constantly reminded her of the legend and what it meant for their family. For the world. Being the youngest, she figured she had years. And there was always the possibility that some other royal witch family would have the honors. Only, that was wishful thinking. "I don't see how me being part fairy has anything to do with it." Saying the words out loud didn't mean she accepted their meaning. However, she wasn't sure there was any escaping it.

"Seriously? That's how you want to play this." He took her hand and pressed his warm lips against the back of her palm. "Ignoring the dust for a second. I believe you felt what happened nineteen years ago."

"What on earth are you talking about? We danced. We were kids."

"True." He stood, stuffing his hands in his pockets, and leaned against his desk. "Believe me, I get how weird it is, especially for someone who isn't a wolf. But I studied for another four months at that studio. While I was in the senior group, and you were with the juniors, you couldn't get enough of me. I would see you come into the viewing area to watch me every day."

"There wasn't a dancer there who didn't, and every young girl had a crush on you." She waved her hand, wishing she hadn't as more fairy particles floated through the air like a magic wand. "But I was five flipping years old. I didn't even know what that meant."

"Maybe not. And trust me when I say, knowing I imprinted on you before I came of age, well, that has made for one hell of an awkward dating life for me all these years, knowing that you were out there, waiting for me."

"Now you're being a conceited asshole."

"Not really. It's just how imprinting works," he said. "Are you going to tell me that you've been spewing fairy dust for years?" He leaned closer. "And before you think about lying, I'm an alpha wolf, and now leader of my pack. I attend local Twilight Crossing Council meetings. I'm bound by paranormal and human laws to protect fairies, wolfairies, and now your sister's twins. I know all about the Legend of the Fated Moons. The four pairings of royal witch fairies and wolves and those wolves imprinted on their mates when they were young." He arched a brow. "It was all predicted in those stupid watcher bubbles, and now the Twilight Crossing Council is doing what they can to protect the future."

Christ. He'd accepted pack leader and she'd yet to offer her condolences. That should have been the first thing she'd done the second she stepped into his office. "Darrell, I literally just learned about your father. I'm so sorry. I know I was only a little girl, but I remember what a kind soul he was." She smiled, hoping some of her healing powers would come through and ease Darrell's aching heart. "He always took the time to talk to me, and he always brought me flowers after showcases."

"In part because he always thought you special, even before he knew I'd imprinted," Darrell said. "And thank you. I miss him terribly."

"He was a good man." A tightness filled her soul. It was deep and somewhat dark. It was as if a senseless black hole had opened inside her heart and sucked out all her blood.

Darrell nodded. "But now you're using that to avoid what your fairy dust means for us."

She jumped to her feet. "I'm sorry, but I don't want that legend. And even if all that you're saying is true, I'm not ready to hang up my pointe shoes, settle down, and have a bunch of wizard and witch wolfairies. I'm way too young. I have a couple of good years left as principal. And then the world is still my oyster. This is all crazy talk. You're good-looking. Actually, you're sexy as hell, but I don't even know you."

"While I don't want you rejecting me, I can't say at thirty that I'm ready for that either, and perhaps it's good that you're fighting this and not accepting me right now because it all might not matter anyway." He rubbed his temples. "I need you to do me a really big favor. It's huge. Massive. But please, I need you to do it for me."

"What is it?" She should have just said no, but she couldn't deny the pull he had over her good sense. It was like she was driven to stand next to him or some such bullshit. And she wanted him to elaborate more on why he thought her pushing him away was a good idea. But verbalizing that question would mean she entertained the idea and that, she wasn't ready to admit to herself.

"Can you tell me what my aura says?"

"That's not my specialty."

"But you are a witch, so you can see my aura."

"I'm not an aura reader. That would be my sister Amanda."

"But you can see them. Peer inside. Check them out, right?"

"Oh God, no. My father can look inside. So can Trask. And they could both see if someone tampered with any aspect of who you are at your core. My sister could, but she's a little gun-shy after what happened with Jackson and nearly dying and all. Plus, now that her fate has been changed in this universe, her role with our coven is no longer that of a reader. She'd actually have to get Trask's permission." She covered her mouth. That information was forbidden to be shared. Trask's visions for the future of the witch and wizard wolfairies were not clear. And they might not be until all the pairings were complete.

Shit. She did not want to be part of this plan.

"I know all about it." He cocked his head. "When I became leader of my pack, I was given the details. But all paranormal creatures know about the Fated Moons. The world saw the two moons hanging in the sky. They assume it's Jackson and Amanda. They just don't know where they are or who the next pairing is, and right now, it's not my biggest concern."

"What is, then?"

"If you can't do an aura reading, can you see them? Does that take a lot to do?"

"No. It would require a little more concentration from me, but I wouldn't know what any of it meant," she said. "Give me your hands." She laced her fingers through his and focused on his energy. On his pulse. She squinted, but all she got was a faint reading. She tried again, but she got the same results. She pulled her hands away. "I can barely see yours and it's not showing as layers like it should."

"Is that normal?" He didn't like playing dumb.

As if he honestly believed his mate would lie, because he didn't. But he had to be certain.

"Well, no. But like I said, this isn't my area. While I studied it in witch school, it was my weakest skill. Honestly, I'm not the best witch at all. I practice every day, as I should. But it's never been a passion like dance is."

"But what you see with my aura now, it's not right."

"I can't believe I'm going to admit this," she said with a scowl. "The last showcase you performed in at the studio, I asked Amanda to read your aura."

"You did now. How adorable."

"Don't make this weird." She tucked her hair behind her ears. "She told me your aura was vibrant and filled with passion and joy, but she saw a gray hue."

"What does that mean?"

"Any number of things. It could have been because you had just exerted so much physical and emotional energy. Or something could have upset you that day. She suggested you could have been sad since you were leaving the studio. It could have even been caused by a cold." She narrowed her eyes. "While auras change over one's lifetime, they don't fade like that. Not even when we're near death."

"I was afraid of that," he whispered.

"Why?"

He stared at the ceiling. "Male alphas in my pack are coming down with the same illness that killed my father. We've had specialists in, and they have no idea what the illness is or how to treat it."

"I don't know if I should say anything, but Jackson mentioned something about your father dying of unnatural causes."

"Chaz Ferguson told me they were discussing all this at the national meeting and would get back to me, but I need answers."

"Who have you worked with in both the human and paranormal world?"

"Human doctors did all the normal tests and it appeared my father died of heart failure. But he was not an old man or had any heart issues at all. So, we called in a witch doctor, who said a black spell was cast on someone in my pack. It could have been my dad, but since he passed, and all his organic energy had already left his body, they couldn't tell." He held up his hand. "But it frightened her so badly she told us all we were cursed. Doomed. And to never seek her services again."

"That doesn't make sense." Avery let out a puff of air. "Any witch doctor can cast a reversing spell. Or at the very least, slow down the process, especially if they suspect it was indeed black magic."

"The witch mentioned something about it being locked."

"All black magic has been banned, but some covens have cursed their black magic, which is also illegal because it has devastating effects and can be irreversible to the person who cast it as well as to those who are inflicted." She reached out, placing her warm hand on his aching knee. His muscles tightened, and a tingle filled his bloodstream. It gave him strength. "You need to find the source of the spell."

"The witch doctor told us we need to find the wolf that carries the cursed spell, but since all high council members, all alpha males, and our pack leader exhibit signs of this illness, she couldn't find the carrier. All she said was that we all had the same single-layer aura, and she had no idea what to do."

"Oh no." Tears welled in her eyes. "Every male is affected?"

"To varying degrees, yes."

"And this witch doctor did nothing for you? No potions. No healing chants. Just left?" she asked.

"Not exactly." He returned to the other side of his desk, easing back into his massive leather chair. "She did give us some healing potions, but all that seems to be doing is buying us time. She told me that the only people who could help me were Toldar and maybe your father. However, she also warned me not to take it to the Twilight Crossing Council."

"Not sure why she told you not to take it to the council, but have you reached out to Trask?" She sat on the edge of the desk. "And you need to know Toldar prefers to be called Trask."

"I've never met him."

"Seriously? He attends the major Twilight Crossing Council meetings," she said.

"My pack doesn't have a seat at the national level. Only locally. And if our numbers keep dropping, we'll need to merge with another one. Chaz has already made the offer." He leaned over and took her hand. "Do you have any idea how soothing this dust feels? It's better than any healing potion that witch doctor gave me."

"I'm told that when a witch is part fairy, the dust can take on the attributes of the witch's specialty. Even though I'm not a master, I'm still a healer, so that's good. Maybe it's helping to slow down whatever it is that is killing you." She choked on the last few words. She never wanted any creature to suffer. Ever. It was against her nature as a decent person, but even more so as a healer. As a small child, she would always try to heal her sister's ailments and broken bones. She reached out and touched his knee. "It hurts here, doesn't it?"

"That's where it started. I thought maybe it was arthritis or something." He chuckled. "Like you, I pushed through the pain for years."

"How many?"

"I can't even remember anymore."

She knelt before him and rubbed her palms together. "Wow. I wasn't going for more dust, but I'll work with it," she whispered. "Where else?"

He curled his fingers around her wrists. "Don't."

"Why not?"

"I can feel you accepting me. Taking a stand by me. You do that and mating will begin. The last thing I want to do is break your heart by having you watch me die." He closed his eyes for a few seconds before blinking them open. "I wanted to be healed before I came to you. To be whole so that we could go through the process naturally. But I need your father's help."

Her heart felt as though it was lifting right out of her chest.

He was right. Her soul wanted to connect even if her mind wasn't ready.

"My dad's at home. Let's go talk to him." She took a step back, focusing her energy on her core and pulling her dust to her center. Reluctantly, the particles shifted in the air and floated into her body. "If he doesn't have the answers, he'll know how to find them."

3

*A*very took the hand that Darrell offered and eased from the driver's side of her vehicle.

"I have to ask, but only because I noticed that guy at rehearsal. Do you always have a bodyguard?"

She rolled her eyes. "That started when Amanda and Jackson got together. Everyone's just worried someone might try to take out me or one of my sisters. But yeah, being part of the royal family means sometimes I'm followed by that big guy."

"Does he have a name?"

"Ollie. He doesn't talk much. More like grunts at me." She pulled open the door. "You can wait in here." She escorted Darrell into the living room near her father's home office. The second she'd heard his voice at rehearsal, her insides turned to a warm marshmallow roasting over an open flame. Her heart lurched to her throat when her eyes finally focused on the man walking toward the stage. She'd mooned over Darrell for years, making sure she had a ticket to see his performance every time he'd come to town. A few times, she'd even managed a backstage pass, but he'd always been surrounded by an entourage, and women fell to his feet, begging for his attention.

She never wanted to be that girl.

Shortly before she'd been cast as the understudy for the New York City Ballet, Darrell had retired and began a career as a choreographer. She'd always hoped he'd land back in the Big Apple.

"I can't thank you enough for bringing me here," Darrell said. His dark hair flowed over the collar of his shirt. It looked like he hadn't shaved in a week, and his dark orbs speckled with almond freckles seemed to carry a burden so deep it touched his soul.

She'd learned so much about imprinting from her brother-in-law and sister. She understood that a wolf had absolutely no control over it. And that when it happened with a species other than a wolf, or even with a wolf, acceptance did play a role.

Amanda described it as consent, whereas Jackson said it was more like taking a stand. Choosing to fight, defend, and love.

Avery couldn't deny the emotions that swirled around inside her belly. They'd been there for years. Darrell had been her first crush, and he'd always been in her dreams. She'd fantasized about being with him and not just sexually. It was always the fairy-tale ending. Part of her now wondered if it was because he'd imprinted.

Or because she really liked the damn wolf.

Either way, her mind and heart were at odds, and she could sense the tug-of-war raging within her body.

"I wouldn't be surprised if my dad already knows about your father and what's going on with your pack. He does attend the national meetings," she said, pointing to the bar. "Care for a drink?"

"I'm good." Darrell shook his head as he inched closer. A warmth rolled across her skin like the sun beating down on the sandy beach. Only, the closer he got, the colder her aching knee felt.

The one doctor she'd spoken to thought it could be arthritis.

The kiss of death for a dancer.

Yet her symptoms didn't present as a typical painful joint.

"I didn't think all this through. I should have known that you were part fairy. I knew about your sister and Jackson. I just never believed we could have been part of that legend." He stood about five inches taller than her five-seven frame. His biceps filled out the fabric of his black T-shirt. He might be on the thin side, but he didn't lack in the muscle department. "I should have reached out to your father on my own. Although, him being a prince and all doesn't make it easy."

"You would have had to get ahold of his secretary. Make an appointment. It would have been a whole thing, even though the two of you have met before. I'm happy to do this for you." She patted Darrell's chest. "I've always thought I owed you one."

"For what?" He stood only inches away, his hand resting on her forearm, dust flying everywhere.

She had to swallow a moan, which made her cough. She cleared her throat. "Making a five-year-old look like a ballerina."

"No need to be modest now. You were the most talented girl in that room, and you know it."

Her cheeks heated. Knowing she was good was one thing. Bragging about it was something entirely different. "There were a lot of excellent dancers that day."

He lifted her chin with his thumb. "But there was only one destined to be a principal dancer, and when we danced, it was like we'd been doing it forever."

"I was five," she managed to say as every inch of her skin sizzled with the anticipation of his lips exploring her body.

"That's part of why it was so amazing. You danced like a seasoned professional. You made me look good." His thumb traced her lower lip as his gaze followed the motion. "Watching you today made me want to leap onto the stage and perform with you."

She gasped. Dancing with him had been a wild fantasy. One she stopped entertaining years ago.

"You're captivating and staying away from you now is going to be impossible," he whispered, leaning in and kissing her cheek. "When the curse is broken, and I know my pack is safe, you and I will dance again. It just won't be onstage."

"Um… oh… okay." She blinked, trying to get rid of the image frolicking in her head of him naked under bedsheets, his hair all ruffled from a night filled with sex. "I should go get my father," she managed to ground out.

Darrell took a step back, shoving his hands in his pockets. "Thank you."

"No problem. I'll be back shortly. Make yourself at home." She turned on her heel, and as gracefully as she could, she scurried out of the living room and down the hallway toward her father's office. She tried to push the idea as far out of her mind as she could that Darrell was not only her soulmate— or in his wolf world, his fated mate.

But they were the second pairing of the Legend of the Fated Moons.

"Dad?" She knocked on the door. Her father, Prince Albert, was a powerful wizard and the head of the royal family and leader of the Coven of the Silver Flock. His duties went far and wide, and one of them was making sure every coven followed all coven laws.

More importantly, they followed the laws of humans and of paranormals.

Most did.

But a few didn't.

Including her auntie Alley, who had cast a blocking and unlucky spell on Jackson, nearly destroying him and almost killing Amanda.

"Come in," her father shouted. "I wasn't expecting you this evening, though I'm quite happy to see you."

Quietly, she closed the door behind her and greeted her father with a hug and kiss. He stood close to six foot four, and his personality was larger than his thick, muscular body. All her life, he'd been her personal hero, and all four of his girls had been the apple of his eye. Neither she nor her three sisters ever felt as though one was favored over the other, though being the baby meant Avery got away with so much more than her sisters.

"An old friend of mine needs help."

"Old? Sweetheart, you don't get old friends until you're at least in your fifties," he said with a laugh. "Let me guess, it's—"

"Darrell Hughes." As a small child, interrupting her father would have resulted in the loss of her cell phone privileges. As an adult, it brought a scowl.

But today, it brought an arched brow and the faintest of smiles. "Is this the dancer whose pictures covered your bedroom walls when you were a teenager? The one you said you were going to marry. The one—"

"Dad, please." She folded her arms, giving him her best 'I'm a grown-up' look. But it did nothing except make her father laugh harder.

"I'm sorry, but for years all you could talk about was that young wolf and you made me take you to every performance he was in when he came to town." Her father ran his palm over his mouth. At least he tried to wipe the grin off his face. "How is it that he's an old friend?"

She cocked her head. "Come on, Dad. We trained at the same studio."

"When you were a baby."

"Not the point and someone cast a locked black magic spell on his pack," she rambled off as quickly as she could, diverting her father's attention.

His grin quickly turned into a grimace. "He told you this?" her father asked. "What exactly did he say?"

"So you know what happened to his father? And what's happening to every male in his pack?"

"This is Twilight Council Crossing business." Her father rested his elbows on the large desk. "It's under a hush order. He shouldn't have said anything to you."

"Daddy, he's the pack leader and dying." Tears stung her eyes. "It could have taken weeks for him to get an appointment with you."

"That's not the point. And this doesn't concern you. He shouldn't have brought you into it."

"Actually, Daddy, it does concern me." She sucked in a deep breath. "I'm emitting fairy dust whenever I'm around him."

"You've got to be kidding me." Her dad slumped back in his chair. "I have accepted that all four of my daughters are part of this legend and part of me is damn honored. But you know how worried I have been about you girls."

"Oh, we know. You wanted us all to move back in here, but Trask talked you out of it so that we could freely roam and our wolf counterparts could find us."

"I agreed only because he put a tracking spell on you."

She shivered. "I hate that. It's worse than Find My Device, but I understand it's for our safety. However, I do think having someone follow me as well is a little over the top. I mean, even Darrell thought it was weird that there was someone lurking in the shadows, watching."

"You've had bodyguards your entire life. This is

nothing new. It's just a little more in your face." Her father lowered his chin and arched a single brow. "So, Darrell imprinted on you. Do we know when this happened? Does he know?"

"Yeah. When I was five."

"And have you accepted? Has the mating process begun?" He leaned back and folded his arms.

"You were so happy when it happened to Amanda. Why is it so different with me?"

"Oh, my sweet child. It's not that at all. I knew it was going to happen sooner or later. To all of you. I had hoped you'd be the last one. You're my baby and you're only twenty-four." He leaned forward and pointed toward the door. "But that wolf out there has the weight of his pack on his shoulders. His father died a couple of weeks ago. And more men have passed. He's slowly dying and we don't know how to stop this. If that weren't happening, I'd be tickled pink by this pairing. But you must consider the obvious."

"And what's that?"

"The Legend of the Fated Moons could possibly go on without Darrell if you wind up pregnant."

"Daddy. I can't believe you just said that. First

off, I have no plans on having a family for years." She gasped as the gravity of her father's words settled into her heart. "Oh God. What you're saying is the birth of those babies is more important than the lives of their parents."

Her father nodded.

"That means that no matter what, I have to accept him and our fate, or none of my sisters and their children stand a chance."

"Unfortunately, that is correct." Her father pushed back his chair, running a hand through his graying hair. "Let's go get him."

She gasped, gripping the doorknob. "He told me to fight and not accept him. Can I really do that?"

Her father rested a hand on her shoulder and gave a little squeeze. "To a certain extent, yes. But you four girls and your wolf mates are unique. Special. What you are going to bring into this universe will change the world. Fighting it isn't going to help him or the future. So don't bother."

"But I'm torn." She rubbed the sensitive skin under her eyes, hoping to keep the tears from rolling down her cheeks. "We're talking about a future I planned versus a future that, while I do someday want, I'm not ready for."

"I know, sweetheart. But we can't change fate. This one is written in the stars. It's what you were meant for and just like Amanda, it will come naturally to you," he said. "I'm going to call Gabe and have him schedule an emergency meeting of the elder and coven council for tomorrow. Bring Darrell back here. I'll leave the door open."

Darrell stood in front of the sofa, staring at the family portrait, focusing on Avery's father. He sat on a bench, his arm around his elegant wife. His children sat in front of the happy couple, all with bright, smiling faces. While out in public, the royal family always behaved as one would imagine. They dressed to perfection with designer clothes and appeared as though they were a bit on the snobbish side. However, whenever he'd seen them in private, like at the studio, they were down-to-earth, regular people.

Even Prince Albert shied away from his title, preferring to be called Mr. Windsor or just plain Albert.

Darrell rubbed his thigh. The last time he had seen his father alive, he'd looked so old and frail.

Whatever illness he'd contracted had aged him at an accelerated pace. But Darrell had still been shocked when he'd gotten the call that his beloved father had died of heart failure.

The ache in Darrell's joints reminded him that what happened to his dad was happening to him.

He inhaled the fresh scent of lilies.

Avery.

He smelled her minutes before she practically danced into the room with all the style and grace that made her the sweetest creature he'd ever laid eyes on.

A trail of fairy dust gathered behind her, rolling into a ball. Both it and she crash-landed into his body.

"Whoa," he said as she wrapped her arms around him. "What's this about?"

"Seeing my dad reminded me of what you lost," she whispered into his neck. Her hot breath tickled his skin, exciting every cell. "And how fresh that is. You haven't had a chance to grieve."

He threaded his fingers through her long, silky hair. Since his father died, all he could focus on was finding a cure. His pack, his mother, and his siblings needed him to step into his father's shoes and lead The Red River Pack during this time of uncertainty. Fear gripped the hearts of all members, and they looked at him, wondering if he was half the man his father had been.

He swallowed the lump in his throat. His father had been his hero. His greatest supporter. And as an adult, his best friend.

"I can't afford to grieve. My pack needs me to find the answers to survive," he said.

Her gentle touch and warm fairy dust helped ease some of the ache in his heart, but it also reminded him that even if they found the source of the spell, he could be dead within the year.

Needing to put some space between them, he took a step back.

Her thick eyelashes blinked over her watery sea-blue spheres as her fairy dust took flight.

It would be impossible to resist her, but he'd have to, at least for now.

She palmed his cheek, sucking him right back in. "It's okay to feel and it would be good for you. Certain aspects of our auras are attached to our emotions. That's partly why readings can be tricky. Feelings affect the outcome. But allowing yourself to feel the pain of your father's death, even in small doses, could help with whatever is going on with your aura layers."

Inching closer, resting his hands on her hips, he dropped his forehead to hers. "I feel it. Every morning, I wake up hoping it's all a bad dream, and then I move. My joints feel like I need a good shot of oil. My muscles feel weak, and it all reminds me of what my father went through. What others in my pack are suffering. I'm their leader. I have to serve them before I serve myself. I will grieve when this is over." He leaned in, but instead of taking her mouth in a kiss that would end all kisses, he brushed his lips across her cheek. "Can your father see me?"

"Oh, yes. He's waiting for us." She took his hand and led him through a long hallway. "I told him about the fairy dust."

"Wonderful." He should pull away. Right now, he had nothing to offer but a broken heart. Instead of taking the new job so he could be near her, he should have gone through the proper channels to get the help he needed from her father and the council. But it was too late to turn back now. "He would have seen this stuff anyway. I gather it's more than safe to assume he knows what all that means and now has a loaded shotgun behind his desk and he's poised to use it."

She laughed. "While he's not overly thrilled at

the timing because I'm so young and your situation, he's taking it better than I am."

"You seem to be handling it quite well, even though you haven't accepted me." He squeezed her hand. "Which is a good thing."

"My father says otherwise." She turned and glared. "And we're not getting into all the reasons why he believes that right now."

"Whatever you say."

"My dad is trying to schedule an emergency meeting with the elders and the witch coven. That means Trask will be involved and that's a very good thing. He's more powerful than my dad."

"I have to admit, the idea of meeting Trask is about as utterly terrifying as going into that office right now." He pointed down the hallway.

"My dad's a big softy and Trask is a sweet-heart." She smiled. "And really hot too."

Darrell growled. "You should know. I'm a jealous man."

"I'll keep that in mind." She stopped at an open door. Her father sat behind a large desk, his cell pressed to his ear, waving them in.

Darrell tugged his hand free as he stepped across the threshold. He'd met the prince before, but he'd been a small boy and Avery had introduced him as her *daddy*. But seeing the impressive man in his light-blue button-down shirt, sitting behind his desk, made Darrell want to shift and run like a scared little pup. The title alone intimidated him, but seeing the tall, muscular man in person terrified him. He puffed out his chest. He never really thought he'd be *the* alpha of his pack, at least not this soon, but it was time he started acting like one.

"Thanks," her father said as he set down the phone, stretching out his hand. "Darrell, it's nice to see you again after all these years, but I'm sorry for the circumstances."

"Sir," Darrell said, not knowing the proper protocol. "Thank you for seeing me on such short notice, but Avery said you wouldn't mind."

"I don't mind at all. Please call me Albert," her father said, pointing to a seat in front of the desk. "Avery, please go get us some coffee and your mother's muffins."

"Dad, I—"

"I need a moment alone with your friend."

Darrell glanced over his shoulder as he took a seat. Avery crinkled her nose, obviously not thrilled about being dismissed. But she nodded and disappeared into the other room, leaving him alone with her father.

"Why have you lied to my daughter?" her father asked. "And your fated mate."

Darrell snapped his head, catching her father's gaze dead-on. "Excuse me?"

Prince Albert stared at him with an arched brow and a deep scowl. "I might not be a wolf, but one of my daughters is married to one. Not to mention my role as liaison between the covens and the Twilight Crossing Council." He held up his hand when Darrell opened his mouth. "I understand that acceptance is necessary in a normal imprinting mating situation. But why are you telling Avery that she can hold this off? Or choose, because that's not how this works, son. And you know it. The only reason it took so long with Amanda and Jackson was because of the blocking spell. There is no such thing with you."

"No offense, sir, but we don't understand what spell or what kind of magic was used. We don't even know who the so-called carrier of this magic is that is slowly killing off every male in my pack." Darrell sat up taller. Alpha or not, her father deserved respect, and he'd give it in spades. "The only thing we know for sure is that I have almost no aura left. My body is weakening. Everything inside me hurts. Though, to be totally transparent, it's eased since I've been coated in that fairy dust. I was going on a hunch that my ability to mate would be lessened as well, and I might be right about that."

"Maybe so, but I have four daughters. I love each one with every fiber of my being. It's my job to protect them from harm. Defend them from those who hate. And support them no matter what," her father said, clasping his hands and resting them on the desk. "I didn't ask to be born a royal or to be leader of my coven. But I am. My daughters didn't ask to be the four fairy witches who will change the world. But they are." He tapped his finger on the table. "Here's the real shitty part about this. If you and Avery don't mate and fulfill the Legend of the Fated Moons? What is to become of Amanda's children? Or of my future grandchild? Or—bigger picture—whatever the universe has planned for us." He arched a brow. "I get you're trying to protect her heart from breaking if, God forbid, we can't stop this. But you'd be causing a bigger ripple effect, and we have no idea what the outcome would be. For all we know, it could destroy us."

Darrell slumped in his chair. He knew Albert spoke the truth. "May I ask you something?"

"Of course."

"What does my aura tell you?"

"Not much," Albert said. "An aura has many layers. Some we can see, and some only a high priest such as myself or Trask could peel back more layers and see beyond. But what is exposed is a culmination of your emotions and your past mixed with the present. With some, there are traces of the future. Take my Avery. Because she's a healer, she also can feel other's emotions. She's not a true empath like her sister Arianna, but her aura gets tangled up in others, for lack of a different way to explain it."

"I'm sorry, but I honestly don't follow."

"It's simple. Avery's aura is generally unicorns and rainbows. She's always been this bright and bubbly child. Full of life, pure energy, and hope. She's always been the kind of kid who sees everything as an opportunity. She can make lemonade out of lemons. But she's also hard on herself. Insanely driven. And that comes out in sharp contrast to the rest of her layers. When you mix that with her ability to heal, which means she picks up the emotional and physical pain of others, it sometimes makes her aura look like a hot mess. Amanda used to hate it when I made her read

Avery's aura. It's the most difficult kind to read. One has to be able to pick out the particles that don't belong there. When she raced out of here a few moments ago, she had thin grayness surrounding hers. I believe she got that from you."

Darrell wished he could see what her aura looked like, but he did feel what her father described. It was as if he'd been wrapped in a warm, fuzzy blanket. It both humbled him and angered him. It would be pure torture to destroy that kind of sensation if he were to succumb to this curse. "I don't like that she could possibly be feeling anything that is happening inside of me." He rubbed his knee. "We don't know when this spell was cast on my pack. Do you think because I imprinted on her nineteen years ago, the problems she's having with her knee and ankle now could be because of me? That she's somehow channeling my pain?"

"Anything is possible." Albert opened a drawer and pulled out a beat-up old book. "This is the royal family's Book of Shadows. It contains a lot of black magic and spells, but nothing like what the doctor describes regarding what is happening to your pack. Not to mention, I've honestly never seen an aura like yours before."

"I'm sorry, I don't understand. My knowledge of witchcraft is limited." Darrell had known many witches over the years, but he'd never grown close to any of them, nor did he comprehend their craft.

"Every coven has a legacy of black magic from centuries ago. We've tried to document all the spells and curses from each one that has been banned. However, a few covens have locked their black magic, thinking it will prevent witches from using it, only it has devastating effects. Not to mention, locking it doesn't actually stop anyone from doing it. Only makes that witch suffer."

"What kind of effects?" Darrell shifted to the edge of his seat.

"Let's say a witch casts a bad luck spell that has been locked, they will suffer tenfold the strength of the spell."

"So, whoever did this to my pack, the same thing is happening to them?"

"That's very possible, depending on how the Book of Shadows was locked and how the spell was cast," Prince Albert said as he let out a long puff of air. "I need to find out more about the spell, and the only way I can do that is by tapping into the inner aura both past and present of the source."

"But we don't know the source. What if it was

my father?" Darrell didn't need to be a witch to understand the implications of what that might mean to his future.

"With your permission, I'd like to start with you."

"By all means. There are only a few alphas left in my pack and they will be willing to do anything. We're only forty-five minutes from here, so I can gather them quickly."

Prince Albert held up his hand. "There is a lot I can find by looking through your old inner aura rings and if you're not the source, I could potentially find it."

"Then what are we waiting for? Let's do this old inner aura ring thing."

The sound of ceramic shattering on the floor echoed in the room.

"No, Dad. You can't do that," Avery said, standing in a pile of broken mugs and a coffee pot spilling its hot liquid onto the floor.

Worried she might cut herself, Darrell jumped from the chair, careful not to step on anything sharp, and lifted her into his arms. It felt as though he'd come home. She was meant to be his, and he would do whatever it took to make sure they had their chance at love.

"Put me down," she said sharply, glaring at him.

He let out a low growl but set her butt gently on the seat next to his.

"I have to do it," her father said, folding his arms. "It's the only way."

"Going that deep in a damaged aura like his could kill you both." She ran her hand over her knee, massaging gently. "There has to be another way."

"What's the likelihood that we will die?" He forced his gaze away from Avery, whose eyes turned a dark cobalt, like the angry waves of the ocean.

"About a ten percent chance for me, maybe twenty for you."

"I'm going to die if we don't do something, so for me, it's a no-brainer, but I'd understand if you didn't want to take the risk."

Prince Albert shook his head. "I've looked at past rings before, where no one else on the Royal Council has, and I have a stake in the outcome. But we could call Trask. He can do it too. He's done it many times. He's more of a wizard than I am." He arched his brow, glancing at his daughter. "Do you have a preference in who does it?"

"I'd rather no one did it," Avery said. "But Trask should be involved no matter what."

Albert nodded. "Avery, call Jackson. I think having a wolf here will be beneficial. Especially one that is connected to the Legend of the Fated Moons."

"If you insist on doing this, I'm calling Dr. Kilby as well," Avery said, still rubbing her knee.

Darrell had no idea why he focused on that movement or why he wondered if her favoring one leg over the other had anything to do with what was going on with his pack.

But something told him it did.

4

"**A**re you sure you want to do this now?" Avery pleaded with Darrell as she paced in her parents' living room. She hadn't been able to sleep all night, much less focus on rehearsal, and it showed when she fell twice doing things she could do in her sleep.

She didn't care that Trask had agreed to come or that the power her father's magic held surpassed most wizards. Looking at a person's memories was dangerous and had other side effects besides death. "We can wait one day for the Royal Council to meet. Maybe they have a different idea? Perhaps a seer could do this."

"I know you're nervous about your father—"

"And you, too." Avery stopped at the end of the sofa, hands on her hips, and glared down at Darrell.

Everything about him made her insides melt and her outsides rattle with a combination of anxiety and desire. The schoolgirl crush she had on him for all those years bubbled from her heart, only nothing about what she felt for him was childish.

No.

Her grown-up body wanted to savor every succulent flavor that floated off his skin. She wanted to feel his strong arms wrapped around her while their hearts beat as one.

"Sit down." He patted the cushion. "Trask is here to make sure nothing happens to either one of us."

"Then why isn't he doing this instead of my father?" She let out an exasperated sigh, plopping herself on the couch. As she bent her leg, the cold, sharp pain, like an ice pick jabbing her joint, ricocheted to her teeth. Instinctively, she grabbed her knee and groaned.

"Did you hurt yourself more while practicing today with Olivia? Or when you fell?"

"I told you. It's overuse and I'm fine," she said, though honestly, she had no idea what was wrong, and today everything felt worse. But it would have to wait until after this performance because she was not letting Olivia have it. Not because she was being a bitch or a prima donna, or any reason other than the opening show belonged to her.

"You're not fine. You're in pain. I can tell. I know the signs. Been there a time or two myself."

She turned her head, lowering her chin. "Nice try, but I'm not letting you change the subject. What you are about to do is dangerous."

"Doing nothing is more dangerous." He slipped his fingers through hers and the damn fairy dust flew from her pores like it was the Fourth of July. His silky skin kissed her palm, causing her heart to thump heavily in her chest. "But I will ask to have Trask do it if it will make you feel better."

"No. My father is insistent that while Trask might be more qualified to look inside, my father isn't as good at dealing with all the things that could go wrong," she said. "Can I ask you something?"

"Sure."

"What did you and my father discuss while I was gone last night?"

Darrell closed his eyes, dropping his head back. "Imprinting. Fairy dust. Mating. Fated Moons. The whole ball of wax."

She bit the inside of her mouth. "Why did my dad ask me to leave? It's not like he hadn't already told me."

"If I said I didn't know, would you believe me?"

She let out a curt laugh. "Tell me why. And don't lie to me."

He didn't get a chance to answer as her father, Jackson, and Trask strolled in.

She freed her hand. Her bond with him grew. There was no denying it. Every second they came closer to this insane procedure, the more she wanted to stand up and fight for him. And she knew what that meant.

Acceptance.

Mating.

Fated Moons.

All shit she was slowly accepting.

Yet still didn't want right now.

Darrell sat up, running his hands up and down his jeans.

"This is Jackson. He's married to my daughter Amanda." Her father carried a small vial in his right hand. "And this is Trask. Technically, he's Toldar, but he hates being called that."

"Only because when people hear that name, they get the wrong impression of me and think of my spirit mother. Not my human one," Trask said. "Of course, they are then reminded of what the watchers told everyone about my mother and her death, so there is that."

"Please excuse my ignorance," Darrell said. "While I've followed along with the rest of the paranormal world regarding what happened with the Fergusons, I have no idea what that means."

"The woman who gave birth to me was human. But I am not," Trask said. "At the time I was conceived, my mother had been possessed by Tara Moonglimmer."

"Oh. I've heard of her and was told she's been destroyed." Darrell placed his hand on Avery's back.

And once again, the room filled with more dust.

Trask chuckled. "She has been. But the world, including many paranormal creatures, don't understand that I was created out of pure fairy magic. Not evil, like Tara, who wasn't even a whole entity. For her, my sole purpose was so she could steal my magic to become her true self. Without my powers, she couldn't exist without a host. Her first attempt after my mother was my mate. It failed because my mate is awesome." Trask puffed out his chest and smiled, waving his hand through the fairy dust. "Avery, you're a healer."

"I am," she said. "Did my father tell you that?"

"No. I can feel it in your dust." He gathered it up in a ball and tossed it right into the center of Darrell's chest. "Your fairy side is much more powerful than your witch side."

Darrell gasped as the dust ball disappeared into his body.

"But we're going to have to teach you to conserve it because it knows he's hurting and while you're fighting your connection, it's pointless and needs to stop." Trask waggled his finger. "Your dust and its magic are still developing and because he and his pack are suffering so badly, it could suck you dry."

Darrell jumped a few feet away. "I wouldn't want that to happen."

"I can use some of my fairy powers to prolong things and help her dust settle down," Trask said. "But it's in her nature to heal. And to protect, defend, and honor you. Not much we can do about that."

"I asked Jackson here because of what you're about to go through; he experienced something similar last year," her dad said.

"When I became pack leader, I was given some details, but I'm not sure I was given full access. Do you mind if I ask what the whole story was?" Darrell asked. "And how it's similar to what's about to happen to me?"

"To make a very long story short, Alfred's sister cast a couple of spells on me to keep me from mating with Amanda. We had to banish them, and it's quite painful," Jackson said, sitting in the wing-back chair. "And then my lovely mate put her father's magic in my hands, and I almost died. Let's hope Avery here doesn't have to do that to you and that the two moons hang in the sky soon."

"Perhaps we should get started," her father said.

But her mind kept playing Jackson's words over and over again.

"Why does it have to be me next?" she asked, staring at Darrell. "And why babies right away?"

Her father coughed.

Darrell pounded his chest.

Jackson and Trask just laughed, like it was funny.

Which it wasn't.

"Are you honestly opposed to having children right away?" Trask asked, wiping his hand over his face, as if to remove the smile. "I only ask because I do understand and respect your feelings. When I met Hollie, the last thing I wanted was for my mate to find me. If that happened, it meant Tara had been awakened and I might have to do the unthinkable and destroy my mate like I did my mother, which isn't exactly what happened."

"Not in reality," her father said.

"Well, no. But my that's because everyone in those bubbles lie." Trask rubbed the back of his neck. "Except my wife. But no one could know the truth about my mother. Or my father. Or me for that matter. Even Hollie had no idea who I was. But the point is, I never intended to have children. Now I have Ali and another one on the way. What's happening now is something that has been predetermined for centuries." He clasped his hands together and a green ball appeared. "The only thing I know for certain is that the wolfairies were the key to freeing all the fairies and restoring a balance that had been destroyed. It leveled the playing field for the good side of magic."

Avery peered inside the ball. A vision of two worlds appeared. One with the wolfairies and one without.

The one without was riddled with chaos and anger.

"The first pairing of Fated Moons and now twins of a witch fairy and wizard fairy is tipping us into something else." He spun his fingers. "A cosmic energy of some kind. Watchers have always believed there are two universes, each with different realms. I understand realms because I can transport myself from one place to the other. It's not easy. It hurts. And if I do it too much, too often, or for the wrong reason, it will kill me."

"Then why do it?" Darrell asked.

"I generally don't. Last time I did it was right before I killed Tara." Trask clapped his hands, destroying the ball. "Our research at the farm tells us that long before history was ever recorded, an evil spirit similar to me cast the world into two universes. The Legend of the Fated Moons, if completed, has the power to pull them back together, unlocking a more stable core. But more importantly, pulling those trapped in a dark universe where other witch and wizard fairies have been trapped."

"That is a lot to take in," Avery mumbled.

"I know." Trask rested his strong, powerful hand

on her shoulder. "And I'm sorry the weight of it all is coming down on you. But the universe wouldn't call to you if she didn't think you could handle it. Just like pairing a Havernite with an alpha wolf who had an attitude problem. Or me with a watcher who knew nothing of the outside world except what she observed living inside a bubble." He arched a brow. "I've learned not to question these things, even when they don't make much sense at the time."

"I suppose it's no weirder than Jackson over there imprinting on a one-month-old."

"Yeah, that was strange, all right," her father said. "We know there is a purpose to your mating. Nothing you can do to stop it."

"And that brings us back to why I'm here. We won't have any kind of a future if I'm dead," Darrell said.

She covered her mouth, hoping to muffle the gasp. It did, but it didn't stop the fairy dust. She sighed.

"Avery, I think it's best if you go to another room. Your mother is in the kitchen," her father said.

"Nope. No way. I'm staying since this does affect me."

"No, you're not." Her father pointed toward the hallway. "If I need you, I'll call you. Got it?"

"Dad, we just went five rounds about him being my mate. I'm—"

"Can I have a minute with Avery, please?" Darrell stood, resting his hand on the small of her back. The familiarity of it melted the anger into tiny pieces of forgettable angst.

"Sure," her father said.

She took Darrell by the hand and led him into the main dining room, closing the door. The fairy dust followed her into the space, wrapping its warm particles around their bodies.

Resting her hip against the table, she folded her arms, even though she wanted to wrap them around him, pressing her lips on his, feeling his velvet tongue twirl around in her mouth.

He was hers.

She was his.

It was that simple.

"Well, now you've gone and done it," he said, holding her gaze.

"Done what?" She cocked her head. Her mouth defied her wishes as her lips formed a small smile.

She knew exactly what he was talking about.

"I want to hear you say it." Darrell pressed his

hands on the back of a chair, his dark eyes pleading with her to express her acceptance.

But she was one of the most stubborn women on the planet. It didn't matter that fated mates were destined to be together, their bond stronger than any others.

True love.

She wasn't going to say it out loud while standing in her parents' dining room. Nope. He wasn't going to push her to do that. It was bad enough she had to go and claim him without even thinking about it.

And worse.

She liked it.

"There is nothing to say."

He arched a brow. "I told you I imprinted. I gave you the where. I've hid nothing from you, including the fact that I can't take my eyes off you. All I want to do is wrap my arms around you and kiss you until you beg me to stop."

"It's not fair of you to ask me to say anything. You've had years to think about how you feel. For all I know you could be in love with me already." She swallowed her breath, clearing her throat. "Based on what I've read." She shrugged.

He smiled, and it made her heart skip.

"Love needs time to develop, so while deep in my soul it's true, we don't know each other very well, and if your father and Trask can figure this shit out, maybe we'll have a chance." He took a few steps closer. The heat from his muscles coated her body. "The day we danced, my life changed. Everything I did led up to the moment I could walk back into your life. The last thing I want to do is break your heart by dying."

"Why'd you wait so long?" She chomped down on her tongue, wishing she hadn't asked the question. It implied she wished he had come for her sooner. "I mean, you could have contacted me at any time after I became of age."

He reached out, taking her chin between his thumb and index finger. "You're the best dancer I've ever had the privilege of being paired with."

"I was five. I'm sure there were other principal dancers—"

He gently brushed his lips over hers like a paintbrush making the first stroke on a canvas. "No one has ever been better than you, which is why I'm concerned about your knee and ankle."

She pursed her lips, knowing it also scrunched her nose. A look she wasn't fond of. "I told you, it's overuse."

"You know there is something wrong, and I fear it has to do with me."

"Why do you say that?"

He ran the back of his hand across her cheek. "Is it a cold, sharp pain?"

She opened her mouth, but no words came out. The frigid sensation in her knee started a few months ago. It came and went, but lately, it had increased in intensity.

"I have that same feeling in all my joints. My father also complained of that same pain before he died of heart failure. We need to find out if what you're experiencing is in any way related to this spell."

"Wait a minute. You imprinted on me while we were dancing, right?"

He nodded. "It's not like I had much control over it, and while it made me happier than I'd ever been in my life, it scared me a little."

"Did you tell anyone?"

"I spoke to my dad about it," Darrell said, dropping his hands to her hips. "But that was on the car ride home. Hours later."

Instinctively, she leaned into him. "What did he say?" A wave of sadness coated her heart. His father would never meet their… she couldn't finish that thought.

"That when it happens that way, so young, it means something important and that you were one special, young woman."

She closed her eyes as he kissed her forehead, circling his arms around her waist. Inhaling deeply, she let his wolf scent of freshly chopped wood seep into her bloodstream. That smell had mesmerized her years ago, but she'd been a child and didn't understand why it made her feel so good inside.

"Wait." She cocked her head back, blinking. "If my pain is from this spell, my father would be able to tell that."

"No. I don't want him to worry about you."

"He's already worried, and he's risking his life and powers for me because he doesn't want you to die. And he wants me to be happy. Besides, this might make it so he doesn't have to peel back your inner aura."

"That really doesn't sound appealing."

She let out a short laugh. "He still might have to do it. But if what I suspect is true, he'll know the right location."

"Still doesn't sound like fun." He grabbed her

by the wrist before she tugged open the doors. "What?"

"Not until you say the words." He leaned so close his lips were less than an inch from hers.

"Why is that so important?"

"Because I've dreamed about this moment since I was eleven years old," he whispered.

She swallowed her beating heart. "I accept you as my fated mate."

His mouth brushed against hers as if he'd lifted her off the ground and twirled her around. It lasted less than a minute but she'd cherish this moment for a lifetime.

"We should get back." She pulled open the doors. She took him by the arm and scurried off toward the living room. "Dad." Her father sat in his big chair, reading a magazine, waiting patiently. "Where's Jackson and Trask?"

"Helping Mom move some furniture around to set up a couple of cribs. She thinks her grandchildren will be staying over, often. I keep telling her until we know there's no danger, we'll be going to the farm. But she won't listen to me."

Avery couldn't wait for her sister to give birth, but she had other things to deal with right now. "We need you to cast a matching spell."

"Why?" Her father peered over his reading glasses. "What spell and why can't you do it? I fear your skills are getting rusty."

"Because I think I'm infected by the spell because he imprinted on me all those years ago."

Her father bolted upright. "Your overuse problems?"

She nodded. She would have some words with her sisters for letting that cat out of the bag.

"Hold hands," her father said.

She held up their already intertwined fingers.

Her father reached for a small box on the coffee table. "Out of the cauldron and into this case, bring a single spell into this space. Cast it back if not a match, but if it is, mix it for a batch."

Darrell squeezed her hand as his body trembled. The coldness in her leg increased. She gritted her teeth as a tearing sensation lifted from her knee, floating into the box. A larger one popped out of Darrell's chest. He let out a low growl.

"I have good news, and I have bad news," her father said as he stuck his finger in the box, swirling it around.

"Is the bad news that what's happening to me and my pack is also happening to Avery?" Darrell asked.

"Yeah, that's bad." Her father set the box on the coffee table and continued to peer inside, moving it around and breaking it apart.

"How? Why?" Darrell asked as he tugged her to the sofa. "She's not a wolf, and it seems to only happen to males."

Her body weakened from the spell, she caved into the soft cushions, rubbing her knee.

"That brings me to the good news." Her father closed the box, sealing a piece of the spell. "First, I can probably match it to the coven."

"Since you have it, can't you do some hocus pocus and reverse it?" Darrell asked.

"It's locked, so no, I can't. But whoever cast this spell did so on the day Darrell claimed you as his mate."

"Someone from the dance studio?" She blinked, remembering all the girls who glared at her that day. Deep down, she knew they all hated her. Sure, some tried to be nice, but during her entire career, others had been jealous. She'd learned to smile, ignore the looks, and block out what everyone said about her behind her back. "That certainly narrows down the suspects."

"It does, but whoever did this is either dead or dying," her father said, rubbing his temples.

Not a good sign when her dad did that.

"Why do you say that?" Darrell asked.

"This spell wipes out an entire bloodline by increasing the aging process. It often takes time to worm its way through the bloodline. But because it was a locked spell, whoever cast it either aged faster than anyone in your pack and is dead or is suffering from permanent aging."

"I don't understand that part," Darrell said, his hand resting on her knee, gently massaging as if he knew exactly where the pain was. "Why cast a spell that will do the same thing to you?"

"If a child did this, he or she might not have known. But their coven would have to because this witch would have immediately aged or died shortly after that, and it would be happening to every witch, so with each death of theirs, one would die of yours."

"Why did it start with my father and not me?" Darrell asked.

"I'm guessing that because it was cast on you, the idea was to make you suffer. Make you watch everyone die, and you'd be the last. But it's also possible this coven found a way to keep the witch alive until recently because it took years for it to start happening to your pack, which means they are probably doing the same thing with everyone getting sick," her father said.

"We need to find this coven and their Book of Shadows so my father can unlock it and banish the spell." Avery thought back to that day in the studio. All the girls. All the names.

"I don't understand why this coven wouldn't do that themselves since they are dying, too," Darrell said.

"They can't." She curled her fingers over Darrell's hand. "Only my father or Trask can unlock a Book of Shadows, and if they were to go to him, he'd have to strip all of them of their powers forever for locking it in the first place. Their coven would cease to exist."

"Wait." Darrell pinched the bridge of his nose. "How can they lock it, but not unlock it?"

"It's our law." Her father stood, taking the box in his hands. "I need to go get Trask. We'll work on seeing if we have enough of this spell that will tell me what coven we're dealing with, while you two get me a list of every witch that was at that studio that day, focusing on anyone who might have it in for either of you. Then we need to find out who went missing, got sick, or is dead."

"Thanks, Daddy."

Her father leaned in and kissed her temple. "Young man, you're staying here until we figure all this out."

"I don't want to put you out," Darrell said.

"You're my daughter's destiny. In our world, we call them soulmates. So you're not." He shook Darrell's hand. "Avery, make sure he's comfortable." He lowered his chin. "Wherever you want him to be is fine with your mother and me."

5

*D*arrell stood in the doorway to Avery's bedroom, though it was more like a suite than your basic place to rest your head at night. A far cry from how he grew up. His family hadn't been poor by any means. However, his ballet classes cost a small fortune. Both his parents worked hard to ensure he had the proper training. Anything the teachers recommended, his folks paid for and never questioned it.

By the time he was fifteen, he spent more time living in hotel rooms.

But he was bringing in a paycheck.

It wasn't much, but it helped.

"Shut the door," Avery called as she dumped

her bag on a chair by a sliding glass door that led to a patio overlooking the pool.

"Are you sure that's a good idea?" He glanced over his shoulder. Respect was a big deal in his family. And his pack. As an alpha—and now leader—it was something that all members were required to give. Most did, though over the years, there was always a rogue wolf or two. His father had taught him that demanding respect would always lead to resentment and possible uprising by another alpha—that a true leader earned respect by giving it first.

Darrell learned that to be true in his pack, as a lead male dancer, and also as a choreographer.

The last thing he wanted to do was disrespect his mate's father.

"You're joking, right? Or are you going to all of a sudden start treating me like a child?" She pursed her lips and jutted out her hip, planting her hand on it.

"I only see the woman you've become." He chuckled. "This was your bedroom as a kid?"

"This room is bigger than my entire apart- ment," she said, pushing open the sliding glass doors and letting a cool breeze from the pool float across the curtains.

"I'm living in a hotel until I find something

between the city and where most of my pack lives." He ran his fingers across the back of the coastal-blue fabric of the sofa.

"Did you reach your mom?" Avery asked.

He nodded. "Everything is the same. No one seems to be getting any worse, yet."

"My dad is wicked smart and a great wizard. He and Trask will have no problem figuring all this out." She pulled out a laptop and situated herself on the sofa. "Come sit. You're making me nuts, and we can't do anything until we hear back from Gabe and the rest of the elders on the witch coven. Trask has already spoken on behalf of the Twilight Crossing Council."

"There are only a few names on that list that I even remember." He rested his feet on the coffee table, keeping his hands in his lap, ignoring the deep-seated desire boiling in his stomach. He always knew he'd come back and claim her as his mate. A year ago, he'd almost done it, but he wanted to give her more time. Even though his parents wanted him to marry and have a family of his own, they understood why he wanted to wait. Why it was important to him that Avery have her career. Their age difference wasn't a big deal. Six years was nothing at this point. But still, being principal of a ballet meant her life in the limelight would be limited. He owed it to his mate to let her shine for as long as it made sense. "What are you doing?"

She tapped away on the keyboard. "Googling the names on the list Miss Tammy gave us. I'm sure they all have some social media presence, except maybe the one who did this."

He leaned over her shoulder, sucking in her peach scent. It reminded him of a dry, white wine on a summer night at the beach with a salty breeze rolling in from the ocean. "I remember that one," he said, tapping on the screen. "She was pretty good, though a little handsy. Always grabbing my ass."

"And batting her eyelashes at you. Not to mention she told everyone you kissed her."

He laughed. Hard. "I was eleven. First time I kissed a girl I was fourteen and it was awful."

Avery jerked her head. "Why? First kisses should be sweet and memorable."

"Yeah, but I was thinking about you, and the girl accused me of having my mind elsewhere. I didn't deny it, so she slapped me."

"I would have done the same thing." She shook her head.

He lifted her chin with his thumb. "And what about your first kiss?"

"I'm not telling you."

"And why not?" he asked.

"Because you told me you were a jealous wolf."

"Oh, I am." He winked. "But I promise to keep that in check because I honestly want to hear this."

She rolled her eyes. "I was sixteen."

"Was he a dancer?" Darrell rolled a few stands of her silky hair between his fingers.

"God, no. I've tried to stay away from anyone I've worked with," she said. "My parents started homeschooling me at seven because of ballet, so I had very little interaction with other kids, except for witchcraft school and my sisters and their friends."

"So, another witch."

"He was, but he was our pool boy."

"Please tell me he's no longer under your parents' employment, because my jealous streak will certainly come out."

"He is not." She tilted her head. "Do you want to hear the rest of this story?"

"Please. Continue." He loved sitting here and talking to her like this. He could listen to her voice all day and night. It was like warm honey drizzled over his favorite treat.

"I shamelessly flirted with him. Well, as best I could. I mean, I had no idea how to flirt, except for watching my older sisters, but he did not pay me any attention."

"I'm glad for that."

"You're impossible," she muttered. "I pranced around in my bikini and he didn't even look. Not even when my parents weren't home. So, one day, I marched right up to him, grabbed him by the face, and planted one on him."

"That's one way to get a boy's attention."

"Only, it turns out he was gay." She shook her head. "Story of my life since my next crush was on Brandon."

Darrell nuzzled his face in her neck. He kissed her sweet skin. "Your mate is not gay and you're the only woman I'll ever desire."

"Let's get back to this." She tapped her computer screen. "Looks like Faza's working on Broadway as a choreographer. I'll have my father check out her coven."

Darrell sighed. "While I don't remember too many names, I do remember that in that class, there were only a couple of solid dancers who had a promising career, but most were at best, good teachers in the making."

"Except Regan Wilcox. She was a snot and a half and one big mean girl."

"Who was she?"

"She was the oldest girl in the class, and it was her last shot, and I took the spot. She never got the chance to dance with you that day. After I went, that was it. The directors had made their decision." Avery shifted the screen, showing an archived image from the dance studio. She pointed to a tall girl standing in the back. "That's Regan."

"Oh God. Yeah. I remember her. We took classes together when I first came to the studio. That day, when I left, she was in the bushes. I have no idea why, but I figured maybe she was smoking or something and thought she could hide it. That girl was weird."

"Wait. What?" Avery's fingers paused, hovering over the computer. "She was where?"

"Remember those big purple bushes in the back parking lot?"

Avery nodded.

"I'd seen her hide back there a few times over the years, and once or twice, I'd see a puff of smoke. I thought it was one of those e-cigs. Gross habit, but she wouldn't be the first dancer to pick up that nasty shit. One way to deal with the stress of it all. But she was the same age as me."

"And you're sure you saw her that day?"

"My memory could be off. But I believe I was waving goodbye to you, noticing her, which gave me a sudden chill, and then I got into my parents' car. With both parents being wolves, they sensed I'd imprinted and we went right into that discussion, so I didn't think too much more about the weirdo in the bushes."

"I got a chill that day, too," she whispered as she pressed a button. "It was Regan."

"How can you be so sure?"

She turned the computer screen. "Because there is nothing about her anywhere. No social media. Nothing except one mention from the studio archives."

He reached for his phone. "Let's call Miss Tammy and see if she knows what happened to her." Tammy had been gracious enough to give them a list of students from that year, so he hoped she'd be willing to share whatever she could about Regan.

"Hi, Darrell," Miss Tammy said as he hit the speaker button. "Twice in one day. I'm flattered. Does this mean you've given some thought to making an appearance, and have you talked to Avery about it?"

"I'm sure we can arrange something in the future," he said, lacing his fingers around Avery's, caving to his desire to feel her smooth skin and enjoy a little fairy dust, although whatever Trask had done controlled how much she produced. "I was hoping you could tell me whatever came of Regan Wilcox."

"Regan? That's a name I haven't heard in years. Why do you want to know about her?"

"I can't really get into that, but I wouldn't ask if it weren't important, and we can't find anything on the internet about her."

"The only thing I can tell you is that she quit when she didn't make the company. Her parents showed up a few days after the audition and informed me that neither Regan nor her sister would be returning. I haven't heard from or seen any of them since."

"Thank you, Miss Tammy. Avery and I will get back to you with some dates that might work for us."

"Thank you so much. I was thrilled to see you'd taken the job with the New York City Ballet and are working with Avery. I wish we had videotaped that audition. It was so moving."

"In more ways than one." He smiled as he pulled Avery closer. "Talk soon." He ended the call and tossed his cell to the cushion next to him. Tracing her lower lip with his finger, he leaned closer.

"Darrell," she said in that soft, sweet voice that started a fire deep in his gut. "I know we're mates. But I don't want to push this too far. Not until we have a handle on all this."

"Shhhh. We're alone, and I want one kiss." So much for being respectful.

She pressed her hand on the center of his chest, her fingers grazing his skin with the kind of heat only lovers shared. Her hair bounced over her shoulder, curling at the ends.

He cupped her chin as her long lashes fluttered over her eyes, sending fairy dust to the ceiling. When their mouths met, his pulse raced as if he'd been running in the woods for hours. She tasted like cinnamon and sugar. He wanted to savor her sweetness for as long as he could.

One kiss.

For now.

"That was nice," she whispered.

"The best."

"We need to call my father," she said, resting her forehead against his and letting out a long sigh.

"I know." Selfishness had been something he struggled with most of his life. He wanted to be a dancer and a choreographer, and sometimes he felt like he'd put his family out because of it.

Now he'd stolen a kiss when they should be racing to tell her father what they'd uncovered.

"You have to know that it's not you that I'm fighting against." She rubbed her thumb across his cheek and then dropped her hand to her lap. "What if I had been dating someone else when you showed up? Or had been in love?"""

"I never owned you."

"But you claimed me as your mate."

"I imprinted. It's more like a promise of a future relationship. But we both know now there's a lot more involved. We were destined to be together. Our souls are connected on a deeper level. Also, you have to remember that we know when we imprint, but when it happens that young, it fades as if it were a dream, until our mate is put in front of us and we realize the connection again."

"What would you have done if I had been with someone else?" Her nose wrinkled.

He fought the urge to bat it with his thumb. "That's a hard question to answer because of my current circumstances. I probably would have left you alone." He waved his fingers through the small amount of dust. "But then this stuff happened and knowing the Legend of the Fated Moons, well, that does change things."

"It sure does." She narrowed her stare.

"There's something else you want to ask me." He ran his fingers through her long hair. "Go ahead."

"If I had been with another man, would I have known the moment I saw you? I mean, I did feel something."

"I don't know if what you felt had to do with coming into your fairy side, my imprinting, or the bigger picture of the legend, but I'd like to believe you would have at least wanted me."

"Oh, it was there. It's kind of always been there," she said as she pulled out her phone and tapped on the screen. Once she was done, she tossed it on the table, set her computer aside, cupped his face, and kissed him, hard.

It was wet. Hot. Sloppy.

And everything a kiss should be between mates.

"Shouldn't we go see your father? This information we found out is important," he managed to croak out.

"He's not here. He went out. He'll call as soon as he sees my—" Her phone rang. "That must be him." She set the phone on her lap, tapping the speaker button.

"Hey, Twinkle Toes," her father said. "What's this information you have?"

"I think we know who cast the spell," she said with a tinge of excitement. "Have Gabe and the council look into Regan Wilcox. I can't find anything on her on the internet, including what coven she belonged to, and she and her sister stopped going to the studio right after I was accepted into the company."

"I'm with Gabe now. We're gathering everyone tonight, so we'll have the witches' register find the family name."

"Do you want Darrell and me to come out there?"

"No. Nothing you can do tonight but get a good night's sleep," her father said.

"That reminds me," she said, untucking her hair from her ear, letting the curls fall, covering her face. "What room do you want Darrell to have?"

"Well, that's up to you," her father said. "But I suspect it would be best if he stayed with you."

Darrell covered his mouth, biting back a cough. While he'd like nothing more than to spend the night with Avery, he never expected her father to offer up her bedroom.

"You and Darrell are soulmates. You need to get reacquainted. It's not like you're the same little girl who lined your bedroom with his pictures and dreamed of being his—"

"Dad," she said with a stern voice. "Not only are you embarrassing as hell, but you're making it worse because you're on speaker."

Darrell bit down on his tongue. He wasn't sure if he wanted to laugh, gasp, howl, or run for the hills.

"Oh, I'm sorry. I guess I shouldn't have told Mom to get the box filled with all those things you used to have in your room because she kept—"

"I'm hanging up now."

"I love you, little girl."

"Yeah, yeah, love you too, Dad." She tossed her phone on the other chair and dropped her head back, covering her eyes with her arm. "I don't know what is more embarrassing. The fact that my father just gave a perfect stranger permission to spend the night in my bedroom, or that he thought it funny to make sure you knew about my crush."

"If it makes you feel any better, I have a box filled with pictures of you from ballet magazines and newspapers, and I even kept the DVR of your live performance last year."

She lowered her arm, catching his gaze, sucker punching his heart. Everything about her made him breathless.

"That just makes you look like a stalker-creep. You're a grown man. I was twelve."

He let out a short laugh. "A grown man who admired a fellow dancer and knew he was destined to love you forever."

Her mouth dropped open.

"I'm sorry, I shouldn't have said that."

She cleared her throat. "Can I ask you a really crazy question?"

"Sure." He shrugged his shoulders. He didn't think any question could be wilder than what had happened so far.

"I've seen pictures and interviews with you and various girlfriends over the years. How does that work? I mean if I was your fated mate and you claimed me or whatever?" Her voice rose a notch.

He swallowed. "Are you asking me if I've had sex with other women?"

She nodded as her cheeks turned red. He found it adorable and endearing.

"I'm going to go out a limb and assume you've had sex with men, so I'm not sure how that would be any different."

Her eyes narrowed to tiny slits. "You knew, or believed, we would end up together. I didn't have that knowledge, so it's absolutely one hundred percent different."

"Why, Lady Avery Windsor. Are you jealous?"

"Damn fucking right I am."

"Why is it when you swear it sounds like candy?"

"I have no idea, but answer the question, wolf." She poked him in the arm.

"I told you I talked to my father about what had happened that day. As I got older, I brought it up a few times. I worried we might never cross paths again and he promised me it didn't work that way. But he also told me that I needed to live my life. And that meant I needed to experience all the things that everyone else did. That meant dating. As time went on, and I became engrossed with my career, the imprinting feeling faded."

"Are you saying you forgot? That's convenient."

"I didn't forget. But I didn't lay eyes on you again until you were seventeen and I was twenty-three. We locked gazes from across the auditorium foyer, but before I could come say hello, remember me, you scurried off. From that day on, I couldn't think about anyone but you. Want to talk about creepy, stalker, old-man shit? The age difference means nothing now, but then, yeah, not sure your father would be offering to allow me to spend the night, even if he did believe in fated mates." The feeling he'd had the day he'd dance with her had been intense, but it was nothing like how his heart pounded out of his chest when he'd seen her at the ballet. It had been his last performance and a week later, he was on a plane to Los Angeles and his first choreography job.

The next seven years had been torture.

"I saw you dance so many times," she said quietly. "When I found out you took the job on the other coast, I went home and boxed up the posters." She closed her eyes, shaking her head. "I don't know why I felt like you were abandoning me, and God, I resented that feeling, so I tried to block you out of my mind."

"I did the same thing." He tilted her chin. "Look at me, please."

Her chest rose as she took in a breath, her fluttering lashes giving way to the orbs that let him into her soul.

"I can't tell you how many times I flew back here just to watch you dance," he whispered.

"Why didn't you reach out when I turned eighteen?"

His pulse sped up. Their bond was growing stronger and more intense with each passing moment. "I knew we'd be together someday, but I didn't want to be a distraction from your career. You're too good and too special, and I know what it means to you. I wanted you, my mate, to experience everything that I had already had the chance to live. I couldn't take that away from you."

"Why now? Is it just because your pack is sick?"

"No," he said behind gritted teeth. "I could have reached out to your father without you."

"Then why? I really want to know." She shifted on the sofa, tucking her feet under her butt.

"I couldn't live without you anymore. When I was offered the job, I thought maybe the universe was telling me something."

She burst out laughing. "I guess maybe it was."

He pressed his finger over her lips. "There is something you need to know about wolves and mating since we've already crossed that line, and I want to respect you and your goals. Although, I don't know how this fits in with the whole double moon thing."

"Are we really going to have this talk before we even go out on a date?"

He nodded. "Once a wolf mates, birth control isn't something we think about, much less reach for. So, you're going to have to shove it under my nose when the time comes. Or go on the pill, if you're not already."

"I can't take that. I get horribly sick on it. The bane of my existence."

"Then when we finally make love, like I said, you will have to remind me. I'll do my best, but it's not in my nature once I've mated."

The sound of knuckles on her door made him jerk. He glanced over his shoulder.

"The door's unlocked," she said.

Her mother stepped inside. "Sorry to interrupt, but your sister Arianna is here, and your father texted. He and the boys will be back shortly."

"Thanks, Mom. We'll be right down."

Her mother stepped out of the room, tugging the door closed behind her.

"Arianna is the painter, right?" Darrell asked.

"For the most part, she gave that up." Avery stood. "She writes now for an art magazine. She's very talented too. Much like my father. His next book comes out in a month."

"I read all his novels." Darrell chuckled. "Are any of his stories based on real life?"

"Well, since he writes in the paranormal world, some of it has a ring of truth, but he keeps all coven and Twilight Crossing Council business from bleeding into his fiction." She waggled her finger. "However, he does draw on life experiences and some of the mishaps of his wizard detective with his faulty magic has actually happened to my dad."

"In this moment, I don't need to hear about any faulty magic coming from your dad."

"Don't worry. It was all from when he was in wizard school." She tugged at his hand. "Come on. Let's go hang out with my sister and mom while we wait for the other men in my life."

"Oh, goodie. I get to hang out with a bunch of ladies. Just how I wanted to spend my night. It's not like I don't spend enough time with a stage full of estrogen."

"Watch it, buddy." She slapped his shoulder. "Or you won't get a chance for the need to remind me about birth control."

6

*A*very kicked off her shoes, tucking her feet up under her butt, and stared across the room where Darrell stood by the bar, nursing a beer, while deep in conversation with her father, Jackson, and Trask, who decided to spend the night.

Darrell's confession had caught her off guard. She'd spent years pining after him yet was unable to bring herself to approach him, even when she had more than one opportunity over the years.

What would a man of Darrell's status see in a scrawny teenager?

Of course, she had a bigger confession she should make. But what would he think about that? No. She couldn't tell him. He'd think she was not only crazy, but she'd probably scare him off.

"What's going on, dear?" Her mother sat in the middle of the sofa between Avery and her sister. "I can tell when something is bothering you." Her mother had always been her biggest cheerleader in life. Her mom had style and grace and a heart of gold. As a human, she came from wealth and power, so it hadn't been difficult for her to ease into the role of the wife of one of the most powerful wizards in all the covens on Earth.

As a fairy, her mother didn't yield any power at all. A few specks of dust here and there. They had all wondered if it would grow stronger as the girls came into their fairy side, but that had yet to happen.

And according to Trask, it might never happen.

"I'm overwhelmed." Avery swirled her wine-glass, watching the dark-red liquid hug the sides. "I have so many conflicting emotions, and I can't sort through them all." Not to mention she was keeping a secret from her mate.

God, that sounded so weird, even in her mind.

"That's why you two need to spend time together. When I first met your father, I didn't understand how I could be in love so fast and so deep in a matter of days." Her mother had been dating someone else when her parents first got together, even though her father tells the story of how he'd been in love with her since she was ten. And perhaps that was true. Their relationship in the beginning had caused quite a scandal in both their worlds, but they were the happiest couple Avery had ever seen, and both believed in the concept of soul-mates, always telling their girls when they found the one they were meant to be with, they'd know.

Avery no longer questioned whether or not she was Darrell's mate. She felt that deep in her core. She knew it to be fact. Not only did she accept it, but she welcomed it.

How that happened in a few days, she had no idea.

"Amanda and Jackson struggled with it, too. They didn't have that sharp connection because of Aunt Alley's blocking spell," her sister Arianna said.

Amanda was three months pregnant, but out of fear for her safety, no one thought she should leave the farm. The place was a damn fortress, even though it didn't look like it. But Trask, Dayton, and other paranormal beings had created a protective shell around the farm. No one was getting in, or out, unless invited to do so.

"I've accepted him," Avery said. "We all know I've had a crush on him forever, so it's not that."

"Then what's troubling you, dear?" her mother asked.

Avery had never focused on the idea of having a family. Or even getting married. That concept was so far off in the future that she couldn't even wrap her brain around the idea. She'd been so driven regarding her dreams, especially after Darrell had moved to the West Coast, that even dating hadn't been something she had much of a desire to do. All that mattered was being the best ballerina she could for as long as it lasted.

But hearing about Darrell's father and the rest of his pack made that seem trivial now.

"I'm worried about Darrell," Avery said. Her entire life, she'd been told there was only one man for her, and she now believed that person was Darrell. Her parents never, not once, made fun of her obsession with him over the years. Actually, if she allowed herself to really think about it, they encouraged her to meet him every time they went to one of his shows. It was as if they knew, but that wasn't true.

"We all are," her mother said with a soft, yet strong voice that commanded everyone around her to listen. "But your father made some headway tonight. We'll get the answers we need and reverse this horrible spell."

"Mom is right. There is no way Daddy's going to let this happen. Neither is Trask. Too much is at stake. For all of us," Arianna said, leaning forward, resting her hands on her lap. "But that only scratches the surface of what's really eating at you right now, isn't it, Twinkle Toes?"

"I hate it when everyone calls me that," Avery muttered.

If her father and Trask couldn't reverse or banish the spell, Darrell could die and potentially soon, as in months or even weeks.

Avery glanced toward Darrell. Their gazes locked. Her breath hitched as they shared a long intense moment.

Living without him would be worse than anything she could imagine.

Not being able to make love to him, if only once, would be just as bad.

"Are you okay?" Darrell's voice bounced in her brain like a ball hitting a wall.

"I must be crazy."

"You're not nuts. As my mate, we can project to each other this way," Darrell projected. *"And you'll be able to*

speak to Amanda like this. And Jackson, as well as other wolves."

"Can he hear us right now?"

The sound of Darrell chuckling filled her mind. *"No. But we could pull him in if you wanted to."*

"Can you read my mind?" she asked.

"No. I have to be invited in. Same way I invited you into my space."

"So, I can ask you to leave my head?"

"Of course."

She lifted her wine and took a big sip. *"But I also could talk dirty to you if I wanted to and no one would hear me, now would they?"*

"Please, I beg of you, don't do that," he projected. *"I might not be able to hide certain physical reactions to that."*

Her face heated.

"You're adorable when you blush."

"Go back to your conversation with my father," she projected.

"As you wish."

"We've been calling you that since you were one," her mother said. "And what is this your sister is babbling on about? What else could possibly be bothering you? As if you don't have enough to worry about."

"Mother, really. For such a smart lady, you often

miss the big things." Arianna cocked her head. "Our little one here has never… you know."

"Arianna. Must we talk about that?" Avery sighed. Sometimes she hated being in a close-knit family of mostly all females. It was great growing up with all sisters. They bonded over everything. They shared everything. And her mother had been their backbone. Their father had often felt a little left out and tried to hone in by taking them fishing, camping, and hunting. Worse, he'd sometimes resort to a spa day.

But he was always there for them, no matter what.

And everyone knew Avery had spent more time chasing her dreams than chasing men.

"Oh. That. Well, it's not rocket science. It's normal. Natural. And honestly, instinctual. But we girls can go into the other room and have a little chat like we used to." Her mother waggled her brows.

"Good grief. No," Avery said. "Besides, I've watched a few porn movies. I know how it's done. And I have a vibrator. It's not like I've never pleasured myself," she whispered. While in public, she and her sisters always behaved as the world expected the royal family to conduct themselves, but in the privacy of their own home, outside of their once-a-month family dinners, they were normal everyday people. However, being that blunt tended to upset her mother.

"Well, good. Then perhaps there won't be any surprises," her mother said.

Tonight, it didn't seem to faze her mom in the least.

"But I'm here if you have any questions and so is your sister." Her mother lifted her glass and took a sip with her pinky perfectly poised.

Freaking wonderful.

"Dad told me that he's meeting with the head Wizard of Witches of the Willows tomorrow," Arianna said.

"Hopefully they can find a way to unlock that spell and banish it." Her mother patted her leg with her other hand. "We all need to believe they can do that."

"What if they went underground and the dark world is protecting them?" Avery set her glass down and hugged herself.

"Then we'll contact the Demon of the Darkness. Wouldn't be the first time your father dealt with that ugly creature," her mother said, pursing her lips, making a face as if she'd just bitten down on a lemon.

"Let's hope it doesn't come to that," Arianna said, scooting to the edge of the sofa. "I'm going to head home."

Jackson sauntered across the room, giving her a hand. "Did you drive?" Jackson asked. "I'm happy to give you a lift."

"I came with the stupid bodyguard my father has assigned to me."

Jackson laughed.

"Call me when you know anything." Arianna kissed her mother and Avery on the cheek, before making her way across the room, where Darrell and her father were still talking.

"I wonder what they are discussing," Avery said, contemplating using her own magic to listen in.

But that would be rude.

"Let's go over and find out." Her mother rose, smoothing down her skirt.

Avery followed her mom across the living room with a pounding heart. Her mouth went dry.

"I'm sorry, sir, but I disagree," Darrell said as she stood next to him, wishing he'd hold her hand or put an arm around her.

Any sign of affection might help ease her nerves.

"You can disagree all you want. You're not going," her father said in a firm tone. The same one he used when he'd ground her for something. "I need you and Avery to stay near each other at all times."

"I concur." Trask lifted a tumbler and took a slow draw as he leaned against the mantle.

"Both of you keep saying that. Why?" Darrell asked.

"Because we don't know what we're walking into." Her father held up his unlit pipe. Her mother had instituted a new rule. No more smoking in the house. She hated the damn thing and wanted her father to quit.

So did Avery and her sisters.

"We have to consider the coven is prepared for us to come," Trask said. "It's best if Albert and I deal with this. We have the strongest magic and the last thing we need is to worry about you or Avery."

"I can tell you're leaving something out." Avery knew by the way her father and Trask avoided giving a detailed explanation that they were holding something back.

"Dear, you should tell them," her mother said.

Her father scowled.

"Tell us what?" Avery glared.

"Please, sir. It's one thing to ask us to sit back and do nothing. But to not tell us why isn't fair."

"That's a reasonable request." Her father nodded. "I was able to deconstruct some of the spell from what came out of the two of you and found something very disturbing."

"What's that?" Avery grabbed Darrell's biceps and squeezed. Her heart contracted, tightening in her chest so hard she could barely breathe. It was as if she'd been hurled through the air and landed flat on her back, knocking the wind out of her.

"There was a binding component to the spell, but I don't know how it works. It wasn't specified. Or maybe it wasn't even cast properly," her father said.

"I've been working on dissecting what we have of the spell." Trask set his glass down. "I can tell you that whoever cast it was an immature witch or wizard." He raised his hand. "That doesn't mean a young witch or wizard. It just means the spell was rushed. Or whoever cast it didn't adjust the cauldron words to meet the purpose."

"I'm sorry." Darrell rubbed the back of his head. "I don't understand."

"Every spell is written generically," Avery said. "That way it can be altered quickly to fit any given situation."

"This was a destruction spell meant to wipe out a group of people," Trask said. "But it's only affecting males. Either the witch didn't know that, or she accidentally altered it that way. The binding portion of the spell appears to be an addition to the spell."

"You mean like it wasn't supposed to be there to begin with?" Avery asked. "Is it possible for others —for witches—to know a wolf imprinted?"

"A seer in training might be able to do that," Trask said. "Or one who has great empathy. Or even one with the ability to see the past. So, yes. It's possible."

"Oh no. That's interesting and not good," her father said, waving his finger between Avery and Darrell. "Trask, do you see that?"

"I do." Trask nodded. "I didn't expect the binding portion of the spell to happen quite like that."

"What does that mean?" She glared at Trask.

"Look at your fairy dust," her father said.

She glanced up, and her dust made a circle

around her and Darrell. "I'm getting used to this happening."

"It's not just that." Her father waved his finger. "Your outermost aura layer just connected to Darrell's."

"We're sharing my aura," she whispered. "How is that even possible? I've never heard of that happening before."

Darrell glanced between her and her father.

Tears welled in the corners of her eyes. Aura is made up not only of who a person is but also carries a part of their soul. Without it, any living creature didn't exist. Separating from your aura meant death.

"Why is her aura doing that and what does it mean?" Darrell asked.

"She's your mate. She'll do what she has to in order to protect you, and right now, the only thing keeping you from dropping dead in a few weeks is her fairy dust and aura," her father said behind a tight jaw.

Avery couldn't imagine how difficult the reality of the situation was on her parents.

Her father looped an arm around his wife, pulling her in tight, and kissed her forehead. "If Avery isn't in close proximity, pulling her aura away, there is no telling how quickly you will die. While I believed it was important for you to be near each other, now it's absolutely necessary."

"Why do I get the feeling there is more?" Darrell asked.

She tucked her head under the crook of his arm, wrapping hers around his middle. "It's sucking my life out of me."

Darrell jerked back, pushing her to the side. "Are you telling me that keeping me alive is killing you?"

"It's not that cut and dry," her father said.

"No. No. No." Darrell shook his head, rubbing his temples. "I won't allow my mate to put herself at risk. We'll separate, so her aura—"

"You can't do that, son." Trask rested a hand on Darrell's shoulder. "She accepted fate, which is why her aura could layer on you. If we don't reverse this spell, she will die anyway. Her aura gives us more time, if we need it."

"Whether we like it or not, he's right, son," her father said.

"I need to get out of here." Darrell moved toward the foyer. His dark eyes were speckled with orange balls of fire. "I need to run. Think."

"If you shift, you weaken both you and my

daughter. If you're away from her for too long, the aura that covers you now will never make it back to her, and she'll die. You both will die. Now, please, we all need you to stay here, close to Avery, and let me go talk to the head wizard in the morning."

Avery inched closer, but as soon as she reached out and touched Darrell, he shot his arms out to the sides.

"So, if I hadn't come here, seen her—this wouldn't be happening because she wouldn't have known." Darrell's words tumbled out of his mouth in a harsh tone.

"Don't do this to yourself," Avery said.

"Can I be in a different room without risking the aura to split?"

"It's better not to have a wall between the two of you," her father said softly. "This isn't easy for me or Avery's mother. We're talking about the fate of my little girl, but it's bigger than that. We have the Legend of the Fated Moons to consider. Jackson's children are at stake. Your pack could be wiped out. I won't let that happen at the hands of black magic."

Avery held her breath, staring at Darrell. His nose flared. The veins in his arms bulged. The anger that seeped from his pores burned her skin.

"Darrell," she whispered, resting her hands on his shoulders. "We need to trust my father, Trask, and the council on this."

"What about my pack? Last I spoke with my mother, things were the same, and no one was getting sicker." Darrell tugged her to his chest, threading his fingers through her hair.

She closed her eyes, feeling the beat of his heart against her cheek. With one long exhale, every doubt that had crept into her mind was gone.

"With your permission, Trask can cast a short-term spell to help them fight the effects they are suffering. It doesn't last more than seventy-two hours, but that adds three days to whatever timeline we are looking at."

"Do it," Darrell said with conviction. "I'll call my second-in-command and let him know, but I want you to consider letting Avery and me go with you tomorrow."

"That's not a bad idea, dear," her mother said. "Especially if you find an anecdote at the source."

"It's too dangerous," her father said, pursing his lips.

"Mom's right. If there is a cure, we should be there." Avery didn't often question her father, but she'd dig her heels in when it came to her future.

"You always take your mother's side." Her father rubbed his temples.

"It's not about sides, Dad." Her father had always been a stubborn man, but he never had a problem doing the right thing, even if it bruised his ego.

"Sir, I mean no disrespect. However, I'm going, which means Avery has to come too. I don't like it any more than you do, but I don't think we have a choice."

"Sorry, Albert. They've changed my mind. Having them near the source is a good idea," Trask said.

"I'll agree, but only if you do exactly what Trask and I tell you to do, young man." Her father waved his finger in Darrell's direction.

"I want to move my pack closer to the source, and if necessary, we need to be able to defend ourselves," Darrell said. While his muscles relaxed a tad, his body remained rigid. The alpha wolf in him threatened to break free, but she could tell the man did his best to remain in control.

"Let's hope it doesn't come to that," her father said, slapping him on the shoulder. "Get some sleep. We leave at seven in the morning."

Avery closed her eyes as her father kissed her forehead, her cheek still flattened against Darrell.

Her mother's warm fingers gently rubbed her back as she leaned in and whispered, "I left the box of the things you collected on your bed."

Avery stayed in Darrell's arms until she could no longer hear her parents' footsteps. She tilted her head, catching his gaze. "I think you're kind of stuck with me now until death do us part."

His lips twitched. "That's so not funny."

7

*D*arrell closed the door, making as little noise as possible. He turned and leaned against the wood frame and watched as Avery set the tray of cheese, crackers, grapes, and wine on the small dinette table off to the right of the sliders in Avery's bedroom suite. For the last forty minutes, Avery had given him the grand tour of what could only be described as a palace.

Fitting, since they were the royal witch family.

He'd walked hallways lined with family pictures dating back generations, and Avery chatted about her childhood and her sisters and answered every question he had with a smile.

But it wasn't enough. If this was their fate, then he needed more.

He needed a lifetime crammed into a couple of days.

"Where are you right now?" Avery asked, offering him a glass.

He took a large gulp, staring at her, wondering what her aura looked like when she didn't have to use it to keep someone else alive. He suspected it danced across the room, touching everyone in her presence with a little drop of happiness.

"I'm wondering what might have happened had I chased you down when I saw you at my last performance with the ballet."

"What do you mean?"

He took her by the hand, leading her to the sofa. "My heart ached when I got on the plane for California. You were too young and I told myself I could handle it. That I'd be back in a few years, but I always wondered if you had been one year older or maybe if I just stuck around and tried to be your friend… maybe things would be different now."

"It wouldn't have changed the spell." She leaned back, lifting her feet and resting them on his lap. "We'd still be facing the same problem."

"But we might have had a few years of getting to know each other before that curse kicked in."

"That could have been worse." She took a lock

of her hair and twirled it through her fingers. "Don't be all doom and gloom. Positive energy ignites auras, giving them energy, where negative—"

He held up his hand. "Say no more." Two large boxes next to the door to the actual bedroom caught his attention. "What's in there?"

She glanced in the other direction and her lips parted. "Oh God. I can't believe my mother actually thought we wanted to see that."

"See what?" he asked, tracing the bottom of her foot, enjoying how her toes curled.

"Dance stuff that either she kept or I did."

"So, you've got my posters in there from when I was with the New York City Ballet as the lead male? The ones your father said you had plastered on your walls."

She groaned.

"I'm flattered."

She jabbed him with her foot. "You should be."

"Let's go check it out." He went to stand, but before he knew it, she was on her knees, holding him down on the sofa.

"I'd rather we didn't."

"Well, now I have to know what is in those boxes." He skirted out from under her and raced to the other side with her following. Laughter filled the room, and for a moment, he felt something akin to hope.

"Why does everyone insist on embarrassing me?"

"I can only speak for myself, but your cheeks turn this flushed red color and your nose crinkles and it... well, it turns me on."

"And that's supposed to make me want to let you rummage through my pile of childhood memories?" She sat cross-legged on the floor, tucking her hair behind her ears.

He nodded, leaning forward, their mouths so close he could taste her vanilla lip gloss. "I want to know everything about you, Avery. I've watched you from a distance since you became an understudy. I flew home so I could attend your first performance. I sat in the—"

"You did what?" She stared at him with wide eyes. Her lashes fluttered in rapid succession. Pink, purple, and red fairy dust floated across the room and landed in his lap like little snowflakes.

"I'd heard you were having your first shot as principal, and I had to see it. I watched from the balcony. You danced flawlessly, and when the crowd rose to their feet, it brought me to my knees." He palmed her cheek. "I almost didn't go back to LA and when I did, I was miserable." He pulled out his phone, fanning through all the pictures with a shaky finger. "I did the unthinkable." He held his phone out, showing her the images from the very end of the performance and in the back hall when she greeted family and friends.

"Oh my God." She glanced between him and the phone. "Why didn't you come talk to me? What do you think would have happened?"

"This." He pressed his lips against hers, teasing softly. A low growl formed deep in his throat. "But I wanted you to chase your dream, and if I pursued you then, you might not have done that because we would have mated. Who knows, maybe the Legend of the Fated Moons would have started with us. I couldn't have been the man who stood between you and the last seven years of your life. I got to live my dreams, and I've seen how dancing made you feel on that stage. All I've ever wanted was to make you happy and being a principal did that."

She let out a long sigh, pulling back. "It's hard to reconcile that you didn't ask me out before your pack got sick."

"I haven't asked you out at all."

She cocked her head and pursed her lips, obviously not amused by his offbeat humor this time.

"I took the job as lead choreographer before my father died. Before we knew about the spell and with your career winding down—"

"Excuse me," she said, folding her arms. "I think your chances of getting lucky were just cut in half."

He'd be lying to himself if he didn't want to ravish her body right now in this very room, but if all he had were a few stolen kisses, he'd die a happy man.

Maybe.

"How old was the principal dancer you replaced?" he asked.

Avery scowled. "Not the point."

"It's exactly the point, and you know it. Even though the pain you've been feeling has to do with the spell cast on me, your body is changing. You are getting older, and Olivia is good. Really good. If someone spent time with her, mentored her, she could spend a couple of years as a principal dancer."

"She's a pain in the ass," Avery muttered. "And she's not ready."

"But she will be. And she could be next year.

Help her make the transition and make your retirement about style and grace, not about being pushed out like what happened to the dancer you replaced. As I recall, after that first performance, she did everything she could to keep you down."

"Gwen was a bitch." Avery glanced away, rubbing a finger under her eye.

When he retired, it was easy. He'd rather be doing almost anything other than performing in front of an audience, where she still enjoyed it. It wasn't just about the movement onstage, but the connection to the audience. He understood that in a different way and he wanted to show her she could still have it, while sitting in the audience and feeling their energy as her creation filled their souls.

Giving her a moment, he opened one of the boxes and pulled out a framed picture.

The one of them dancing.

In full color.

He tapped his finger against his chest. "I want to dance with you again," he whispered, emotion choking his throat. He didn't want to be onstage or have anyone watching. He just wanted to glide across the wood floor in an effortless motion of love. "I want to choreograph with you. We could do a year together at the ballet and then create our own company together. Open a studio together. If I live that long."

"Stop making those kinds of comments." She slapped his shoulder. "You think that's what I should do? Hang up my pointe shoes and teach?" She gave him a scathing look as if he'd just cut the bottom of her legs off.

She'd totally missed his desire, but that too he understood.

He arched a brow. "Being a choreographer is a very different job than a teacher, not that there is anything wrong with the latter, but it takes vision and a deeper understanding of the art to do the former. Any one of those girls who never made the company could have easily become teachers, but, like being the one principal dancer, very few could make it as a choreographer."

She let out a puff of air, slumping her shoulders. "I didn't mean it that way."

"I know," he said, setting the picture of them aside, twisting his body so he faced her directly. "I'm not saying you should quit right now. Finish the season, but then think about working with me, if we're still kicking—"

"I'll think about it if you stop talking like that."

With his hands on her thighs, he stared into her

ocean pools of blue and green. Her eyes were an invitation to her spirit and he planned on jumping in. "Okay, but I need to say one thing."

"What's that?"

"I'm a selfish bastard, and I want you, even if it's only for a short period of time. I want to know what it's like to be with you in every way. That might be wrong and we probably shouldn't, but that's how I feel."

The corners of her mouth drifted up into a heart-melting smile. "I'd say if we didn't take advantage of the time we do have, we'd be waving our middle finger at fate, and you know, karma, it's a bitch."

"We don't want to upset karma," he mused, melding his mouth against hers, drawing her tongue in, swirling and tasting her sweetness. His biceps tensed under her tender touch. He tried to bite back a groan as he lifted her into his arms. The ache in his joints had eased, but he knew that was temporary.

"Put me down," she whispered into his neck, plastering him with soft kisses. They danced over his skin, spreading a blanket of future promises across his body.

"I will, on the bed," he said, carrying her across

the room, ignoring the little tickle in his brain that reminded him their time could end in a few short months. Or weeks. Maybe days.

Gently, he laid her on the plush light-green comforter. He drizzled kisses on her cheeks and nibbled on her earlobes. Her thin body hid her strong, lean muscles created from years of training. A ballerina's body was deceiving, not that he'd ever seen one naked. He'd shied away from anyone who reminded him of Avery, which left him sexless in the last three years.

Not that he minded. His dreams were filled with visions of Avery. He'd completely given his heart at his last performance when he'd seen her in the lobby.

He untucked her shirt from her formfitting jeans, her stomach quivering under his fingertips. As he raised it higher, she lifted up on her elbows, then pushed to a seated position, tugging the thin fabric over her head, revealing a lacy white bra. Her tiny mounds peeked out over the fabric.

His throat tightened as his breath came out in a short pant. His pulse raced. He'd been with beautiful women, but never one he loved.

Could he say the words now?

No. It was too soon, even for him. While he felt

it deep in his core, they needed time, which they potentially had little of, but still, it was better to wait.

He unhooked the front clasp of her tiny scrap of fabric and tossed it aside while he stared at her with pure admiration and love. Her hair curled over her shoulders, just above her tight nipple.

Everything in the background faded to a blur. Nothing existed but her and this moment. He could only hope he'd be the kind of man she needed.

Wanted.

Desired.

He traced a path from her navel to her areola, which puckered as she sucked in a breath and bit her lower lip. Her chest heaved out into the palm of his hand. Her soft skin felt like warm oil gliding over his body. Bending over, he sucked her nipple into his mouth. It felt like he'd been given a little piece of heaven.

Her fingers dug into his scalp as he let out a wild moan, which only reminded him that his pants had become a bit crowded.

Running his hands down her back, cupping her ass, he parted her legs, lifting her to his waist, letting her feel the magnitude of the effect she had over him.

He lowered her back to the bed, kissing her other nipple, scraping it with his teeth. She rewarded him with the rolling of her hips and louder groans.

"Let's get you out of these pants," he murmured.

"Only if we can get you out of yours."

"I won't argue with you about that." He fumbled with the button of her jeans and then yanked them down to her ankles. Once again, he found himself staring at Avery. Not just her nakedness but the woman inside. The kind soul he knew her to be.

"Your turn," she cooed, her petite fingers curling inside his jeans.

He ripped off his shirt, tossing it across the room.

Her lips sizzled on his chest as her hands worked on his zipper. He growled behind gritted teeth as she pulled him from his pants, stroking softly. Her fingers glided across him like a conductor, bringing the orchestra to that pivotal moment in the music where emotions exploded.

In his dreams, she always came to him filled with need and desire.

This was better than anything he'd ever fantasized about.

She looked up at him, lashes fluttering over her lust-filled eyes. Her pink tongue flicked over his tip.

"Have you ever pictured me in your mind doing this?"

He watched himself disappear into her hot mouth. "It was nothing like this," he whispered, barely able to form words. He fisted her hair, tugging gently, keeping her from robbing him of what little control he had left.

She rolled his jeans over his hips.

He took her hand, wrapping her fingers around his hard shaft before taking her nipple and twisting it, running his thumb over it as it tightened even more.

She cupped him and took all of him in her mouth. Her tongue twisted and twirled over his sensitive skin.

"Jesus Christ. Where the hell did you learn how to do that?" he asked, dropping his head back. "Don't answer that." He shut his eyes tight as a deep howl bellowed in his gut. He gripped the comforter with one hand and fisted her hair with the other. His muscles tightened, and with every breath, his lungs burned with the purest of passion.

She licked him like he was her favorite ice cream, and if he wasn't careful, he'd melt all over her.

"Stop," he commanded, tugging her hair a little too harshly.

Lifting her head, she smiled, her eyes glistening with the power she knew she held over him like a jib sail catching the wind, hurling the boat forward.

"A little more than you can handle?"

"You could say that." He draped her body over his, kissing her mouth wildly, his tongue in search of her soul. Of everything that made her the most incredible woman the world had ever seen. The fact that fate had deemed him worthy of her humbled him.

He rolled her to her back, settling his face between her legs, inhaling an intoxicating scent that reminded him of coconut milk. He made no effort to tease and toy. Instead, his mission was to satisfy in the most primal way. His lips kissed. His tongue swirled and flicked. His fingers stroked and pinched.

Her hips rolled with his movement, and her fingers dug into his scalp, encouraging him to go deeper.

Harder.

Faster.

"Oh, yes," she said with a panting moan. "Mmmmmmm."

Wanting to see her face, he knelt between her legs. Two fingers glided in and out while he rubbed his thumb over her hard nub. His own release meant nothing without her climax.

"Yes… Oh God," she said, her head bobbing back and forth as she clutched her breasts. Her body jerked and bucked as her legs drew closed, drenching his hands with lust, desire, and the purest form of love.

With a surge of urgency, he guided her legs open, his featherlight touches loving yet insistent. "Don't stop. Keep it going," he whispered, thrusting himself into her with a hard, powerful stroke. He paused momentarily, heaving in a deep breath before pushing a little deeper.

She was so tight.

Too tight.

"Avery," he whispered. "Are you okay?" He stared at her beautiful face.

Her eyes were closed, and she bit down on her lower lip. She grabbed his ass and raised her hips, wincing.

All the air in his lungs flew out like a bird taking flight. "Oh, my sweet Avery." He fanned her cheeks as he pulled back a little, easing himself slightly farther in as gently as he could. "Open your eyes."

She refused him. Instead, she raised her hips, grinding against him and making a noise that was a cross between pleasure and pain.

He kissed her tenderly. Lovingly. He moved inside her slowly. Never going too deep. That would come soon enough. She needed a little time to adjust. And she would. But right now, he hated that he hurt his mate. It wasn't a bad hurt. He knew that. There was enjoyment in their lovemaking. "Please, Avery. Look at me."

She blinked open her eyes.

"Do you trust me?"

"Yes," she whispered.

He rolled to his back, giving her total control of the pace. Of how much she could take in. The only thing he wouldn't let her get away with was not experiencing another orgasm through the act of sex.

That would be a real travesty.

Her first time shouldn't be about getting through the uncomfortable part, even though that was necessary. But she should still have all the joy.

He reached up with one hand and toyed with her tight nipple. His other hand squeezed her hip, guiding her to him and encouraging her to find her rhythm. To find what felt right for her, because this wasn't about him.

Soft moans fell from her lips as she rocked back and forth, slowly accepting his entire length into her body. "Oh my..." She held his gaze. Her movements became wild. Frenzied. She dug her nails into his chest, clawing at his skin. "Darrell," she whispered. "Yes, yes, please," she begged.

He found her hard nub and rubbed it with his thumb while he jerked his hips upward, praying he wasn't hurting her anymore. But with the wild sounds escaping her lips, he highly doubted that.

He couldn't maintain control if he tried. So he didn't. His entire life came down to this tiny sliver in time. The idea that the rest of his life with Avery could be cut short angered him, but it also made him want to savor every second he had with her.

And her family.

"Avery," he whispered as his release exploded in her heat. He thrust inside her, trying to swallow his howl that could wake the dead. She did things to him no woman had ever been capable of and it wasn't physical.

However, that turned out to be a really wicked side effect.

She collapsed on his chest. He wrapped his arms around her body and sucked in a deep breath, spent from the most mind-blowing experience he could have ever imagined. It was bigger than the first time he'd gotten a standing ovation for his choreography. Everything he'd done in life had led him to one place.

One person.

Avery.

She rolled to the side and he held her close, running his hand up and down her arm.

"You should have told me." He tilted her chin, forcing her to look at him. "I would have done things differently."

She blinked out a tear. "And that's why I didn't say anything. It would have weirded you out."

"Don't cry, sweetheart. I'm not upset by it. I just wish you would have clued me in, especially after we talked about it. I mean, you led me to believe that—"

"No. You assumed. And besides, do you have any idea what it's like to be a twenty-four-year-old virgin? I mean, how pathetic." She groaned, burying her head in his chest.

"Well, the good news is you're not a virgin anymore."

"I'm not in the mood for your weird humor, Darrell."

He chuckled, but she was right. His humor was off-color and inappropriate, even if it was funny. "It's not pathetic. I certainly didn't care. I mean, I did. I do." He ran his fingers through his hair. He was tripping over his words and if he wasn't careful, she was going to kick him right out of this bed. "A big part of me is super glad you've never been with another man before. I wasn't kidding when I said I can be a jealous wolf. The only thing that would have changed by you telling me you'd never had sex before is I wouldn't have been so harsh right out of the gate. That hurt you and I could have been a little softer about it. But it wouldn't have changed me doing it. I love you. I want to be with you. You're the only woman for me."

"Oh my God. It can't be."

"Too soon?"

She yanked the sheet around her body and jumped from the bed.

Well, that didn't go over well.

He sighed as he found his boxers and hiked them up to his hips. He followed her to the sliding glass doors. His jaw dropped open. "You've got to be kidding me." He stared at the double moon hanging low in the sky. While it was a beautiful sight with both moons glowing bright, electrifying the dark sky, the last thing he needed to worry about was the fact his mate was carrying his child.

And everything that meant.

Or the fact he might not live long enough to meet his child—children—if the legend held true and twins were really what was predicted for the second pairing.

"I hope my parents are sound asleep in bed and don't see that." She wrapped her arms around him, resting her head on his shoulder. "I really don't feel like dealing with their smirks or snide remarks in the morning."

"Neither do I," Darrell mumbled.

"I'm not going to make it through the entire season as principal now, am I?"

"No. You're not," he said. "I want you to know my intention was not to get you pregnant. I just wanted to give you an orgasm or two."

"Well, you achieved all those things." She patted his chest. "I might have lost my mind, but I might want a few more of those in the morning." She raised up on tiptoe and kissed his cheek. "I'm not saying this because of the moons. Or what that means. I'm saying it because I feel it in my soul. I know we're connected. We always have been. I love you. I have for a long time. I get the whole imprinting thing. I believe it's true. As is the fated mates. But I would have loved you without it."

"You're going to make this werewolf cry." He kissed her temple. "I don't know if that's your phone or mine. But one of them, or both, is buzzing like crazy."

"I don't know about you, but I will ignore it." She turned and headed toward the bed.

"Sounds like a solid plan." Part of Darrell was elated with all that had transpired.

He had his mate.

She was his. They were going to be a family.

As long as he didn't end up six feet under.

8

*A*very blinked open her eyes. Her arm was draped over Darrell's strong middle. She brushed her hair from her face, noticing he was already awake, propped up on the pillows, with his cell in his hand.

"Good morning, beautiful." He leaned over and kissed her forehead.

"What time is it?" Running her fingers across his bare chest, she inched closer, shameless, aware they were both naked. She'd spent the entire night in a man's arms. In Darrell's arms. She'd dreamed of this day for so long. Even after she'd tried to rid him from her thoughts when he'd moved to the West Coast, he managed to worm his way to the front of her mind.

It had always been Darrell.

It was one of the many reasons she'd never been able to bring herself to be with another man. She'd had opportunities. It wasn't like she hadn't done things. But when it came to the act of sex, she couldn't do it. She told herself her career had to be front and center. She'd seen more than one ballerina have to make the tough choice between leaving the stage to have a child or having an abortion.

While she wholeheartedly believed in the woman's right to choose, abortion wasn't something she thought she could ever do, which is why she never put herself in that position.

The vision of the two moons danced in her head. She knew exactly what that meant. It had happened to Amanda, and now it was happening to her. It was fate. Destiny. She couldn't have stopped it if she tried.

Truth be told, now that it was a reality, a warmth had settled through her body. A greater sense of purpose and love filled her soul.

"A little after five," Darrell said.

"What are you looking at?" She scooted closer, resting her head on his shoulder.

"Text messages from my mother asking how you're feeling. Another from my second-in-command asking me if I saw the double moon." He shifted his gaze. "He has no idea that it could be because of me and he wants to know if I know anything about it."

"Wonderful," she muttered.

"Oh. It gets better." He waved his cell. "All your sisters have messaged a nice congratulations text. Not sure how they got my number, but all have mentioned that they tried to reach you last night and this morning and have asked me to tell you to call them."

"Ugh." She buried her face in his neck.

"Your mother and father have also reached out, but they at least had the decency to wait until about a half hour ago. They did say they texted both of us and wanted us to know breakfast would be ready no later than six."

"At least they didn't mention the moons."

Darrell shifted, setting his phone on the nightstand. "Oh, they let me know they saw them. Something about how romantic the night sky was last night and that they were glad we are living and not dwelling on the black magic spell."

"That sounds like my mother. I can't picture my father leaving it at that."

"He didn't," Darrell said. "He reminded me

that I better do things his way today because he didn't want to deal with a daughter who had a broken heart and two grandchildren who didn't have a father."

"Yeah. That sounds more like my dad." She tilted her head and ran her hand down his taut stomach. It twitched under her touch.

He grabbed her wrist. "What do you think you're doing?"

"Relieving your morning tension." She smiled, lowering her hand and gently brushing her fingers over his tip.

He growled, low and deep. "And what would you know about that?"

"I might not have had sex until last night, but that doesn't mean I was totally inexperienced. I know things. Did things."

He pressed his finger over her lips and scowled. "I'm well aware of how good you were at certain things." He arched a brow. "But I never want to hear about your past experiences. I told you I am a jealous wolf. I'm serious about that."

"I can be that way too, but I want to know something."

"What's that?"

"Before last night, when was the last time you had sex?"

He kissed her nose. "I'm not having this conversation with you."

"Yes, you are." She sat up, letting the sheet pool to her waist.

He raised his arm, but she batted his hand away before it could reach her breast. "If you want these." She cupped herself. "You're going to answer my question." She reached under the sheet and gripped him. Hard. "And if you want me to take of this. You'll answer a few more."

"You're going to use sex as a weapon?"

She nodded.

"That's just mean." He chuckled, shifting to fluff the pillows. "Fine. But you can't get mad at me."

"I can if I want. Now talk, wolf."

"That is so hot."

Playfully, she slapped his shoulder.

He chuckled. "I thought I already told you. It was three years ago."

Her lips parted. She'd been prepared to clamp down on her emotions. To hear that it had only been a few months ago. That he'd been taking care of his physical needs because that's what men do.

But three years?

That was not what she expected to hear.

"Really?"

"There is no point in lying to you, especially about this." He took her hand and kissed her palm. "Are there more questions, or can we move on? I don't know how long I can sit here, staring at you, and not make you call out my name while I cover your mouth because you can be loud and someone might hear."

She swallowed. "Why so long?"

He sighed. "There wasn't anyone I wanted to be with."

"And before that?"

"Really, Avery? Why do you want to know this?"

"It's important to me. So please. Answer my question."

"I don't know. Maybe six months or so before that." He pressed his hand over her mouth. "And before that, a year, I think. To be honest, after I saw your performance when you were seventeen, being with other women was like cutting off an appendage. It felt like I was cheating on you. It hurt my heart and it wasn't fair to any of the girls I took out. After the last one three years ago, I figured I could live without it, and it wasn't that hard. Actually, it was easy. All I wanted was you anyway."

"Was I worth it?"

"I kind of wish I had been a thirty-year-old virgin."

She laughed, ripping back the covers and exposing his naked body. God, he was so gorgeous. She'd seen men in their birthday suits before. Experienced oral sex. And she wasn't overly shy about her body, even though as a dancer, she was about as flat as a pancake. Even so, she felt like a sexual woman. Believed she was pretty. Maybe even a little sexy in the eyes of some men.

But the way Darrell's eyes smoldered over her skin, he saw more than her outside beauty.

He saw all of her. Every inch, inside and out.

Licking her lips, she ran her hands up his thighs, digging her nails into his solid muscles.

"I feel like a piece of meat," he said between ragged breaths.

"You kind of are." She leaned over, cupping him firmly, bringing her mouth to his tip. She kissed him. Softly at first. Dotting her lips up and down him while he growled and moaned.

He twisted her hair in his fist. His hips lifted slightly anytime she'd pull away.

She loved teasing him and bringing him the kind of pleasure only she could give. Parting her lips, she sucked him deep into her mouth. She took him as far as she could before easing back to the tip and repeating the motion. Slowly. But with each pass, she picked up the pace and his grip on her hair tightened.

"Avery, you need stop."

Wiping her lips, she lifted her gaze.

"Come here," he whispered, pulling her to his chest. He rammed his tongue inside her mouth. It was wild and reckless. Passionate and tender at the same time. His hands roamed her body, finding every spot that made her a sexual woman.

"Take me," she projected. *"I want you. Need you. Please."*

He cupped her face, fanning her cheeks, staring into her eyes with love and devotion but also a questioning gaze.

"No holding back. Show me I belong to you," she whispered.

"I don't want to hurt you." He kissed her nose. "The first few times need to be delicate."

"I see the desire in your eyes. I feel the passion coming from your heart." She pressed her hand in the center of his chest. "You don't want delicate, and neither do I. That's not who we are. If you're hurting me, I promise to tell you, but I want you to take me the way you've always wanted. The way you've dreamed about. Fantasized about."

He flipped her onto her back, yanking her to the edge of the bed as he knelt before her, draping her knees over his shoulders. "If you're uncomfortable at all, you must tell me."

"You'll know." She propped herself up on her elbows and watched as he kissed the inside of her thigh. His hot breath tickled her skin.

"You're so beautiful," he murmured before lapping at her softly.

She jerked her hips, wanting more. Demanding more.

But all he did was tease and torture until suddenly, he rammed two fingers deep inside.

She arched her back, tossing her head to the side, letting out a moan that bounced off the walls.

Reaching up, he covered her mouth. "Shhhhh. Not so loud." He removed his hand, resting it on her breast. He pinched and twisted her nipple, tugging at it relentlessly. His fingers plunged into her heat like a rocket. His tongue flicked over her sex and her womanhood throbbed, begging for release.

"Oh my God. Darrell. Yes," she cried out.

Suddenly, he lifted her from the bed.

"What are you doing?" She blinked. Her system was shocked by the sudden withdrawal of his hands and mouth.

"Taking you as you asked," he said with a deep growl in his voice. He kicked open the bathroom door and set her feet on the floor in front of the vanity. He bent her over, staring at her in the mirror. His large hands covered her breasts before gliding down her stomach. "Remember what you promised."

She nodded, trying to catch her breath, but it was impossible.

He spread her legs, positioning himself between them, all while holding her gaze. He eased into her slowly, stopping only when he'd reached his limit. "Are you ready?"

"Yes," she whispered.

"Brace yourself."

She gripped the vanity, unable to take her eyes off him.

He gripped her hips, pulling almost all the way out, and then he thrust so hard and fast she nearly fell into the vanity. "Are you okay?"

"Don't stop," she managed as she planted her feet firmly on the tile floor.

He repeated the movement. Slow and methodical but powerful. It was hard and deep. It took all her strength to stay standing. But it certainly didn't hurt. No. It was the most magnificent thing she'd ever experienced.

Her chest heaved up and down with each short, choppy breath as he pounded himself inside her with powerful strokes.

He reached around and rubbed his finger against her, bringing her even closer to the edge.

Her moans grew louder. Bolder. And a few times, he thrust so hard, her toes lifted right off the floor.

"Darrell. Oh. Yes. Yes. Yes," she cried.

His hand clamped over her mouth just as her body shivered with the purest form of pleasure. It rolled over her like a tidal wave and it was relentless. It wouldn't stop.

A low growl filled her ear as his climax exploded.

She slumped back into his tall, strong frame, resting her head on his shoulder, trying to suck in a deep breath, but it was impossible.

His hands smoothed across her flat stomach as he kissed her neck. "Are you okay?"

"I'm wonderful."

He chuckled. "I'm glad." Gripping her shoulders, he turned her, lowered himself, and kissed her middle. "We need to talk about what's going on in here."

"No, we don't." She tilted his chin with his index finger. "At least not today we don't."

"I might not be around long enough to see these little ones be—"

"If I don't get that piece of my aura back, I won't be either." She took him by the arms, forcing him to stand. "One thing at a time. First, we deal with the coven that did this and reverse the effects. Then we deal with the fact you probably knocked me up and that maybe, I might be able to do opening night."

He arched his brow.

"I'm doing opening night." She planted her hands on her hips.

"We're having an argument in the bathroom, naked, after wild sex. Do you have any idea how hot that is?"

She poked him in the chest. "You can't avoid

this with deflection. And me dancing in the first few months isn't going to hurt the babies."

"That's not my issue," he said. "Why is Amanda living at the farm?"

"For safety reasons."

He kissed her cheek. "I rest my case."

"You're so infuriating." She stomped her foot and marched out of the bathroom. She hadn't thought about that aspect of their situation. Or the idea that she might have to go spend the next nine months living in Vermont, hiding from crazies who wanted to kill her and her babies.

She paused in the middle of her bedroom.

Holy shit.

She was pregnant.

With Darrell Hughes' babies.

Fucking twins.

Twins that would change the world.

Well, she did say she missed her sister, Amanda.

9

*a*very slipped from her bedroom suite and made her way down the staircase toward the kitchen where her nose was assaulted with all the wonderful scents that came with visiting her parents.

Bitter brew, cinnamon, maple syrup—not the processed stuff. Fluffy sourdough bread that had to be soaked in egg and baked in the oven. Her mother always stayed up, making that treat for the family when they gathered. Crisp bacon sizzling in the frying pan brought her back to simpler times when she and her sisters were children.

Avery had never wanted for anything and that included love and affection. Her parents were kind and supportive. But they also taught their daughters the value of being strong and independent. Her father had wanted his girls to be able to take care of themselves, not rely on a man. He saw nothing wrong with being traditional. The royal family was full of out-of-date traditions, and they went through the motions of every single one of them. Her family believed it was important to carry on those traditions, even if they were only in ceremonies.

But that didn't mean Avery and her sisters couldn't be or do anything they wanted.

Avery rounded the corner into the massive kitchen. Her father stood over the stove, tending to the bacon. The one thing her mother trusted him to do and not screw it up.

"Good morning, Dad," Avery said as she poured herself a cup of steaming hot coffee. She smiled even though she suspected her cheeks were red. Being with Darrell had been the most natural thing in the world. Even waking up with him in her childhood bed felt normal.

Having wild morning sex in her bathroom didn't feel strange at all.

Seeing her dad shortly after?

Not so much.

"Where's Darrell?" her father asked as he placed a few bacon strips on some paper towels.

"Just getting out of the shower. He'll be down in a minute." That's two sentences she never thought she'd say.

To her father.

In her parents' home.

Heat flushed from her head to her toes.

"How are you feeling this morning?"

She burned her throat as she swallowed the scalding liquid, trying to cover a cough. "Just peachy."

"I'm glad to hear that. Your mother and I were getting worried because you didn't answer our messages." He plopped a piece of bacon in his mouth and smiled. "Darrell was kind enough to, but it would have been nice to hear from my child."

She'd seen Darrell's text and it hadn't said much. Only that they were awake and would be down shortly.

"Want to talk about it?" her father asked.

Sometimes coming from a close-knit family sucked. She remembered when her sister Amanda had moved in with Jackson so they could protect each other from black magic. Her father had the nerve to bet how long it would take before they were sleeping together.

He won that bet. But it hadn't been a fair wager.

He had more information than her and the rest of her sisters. Had they known about the imprinting, they might not have believed it would have taken longer, if never.

"I do not."

The oven timer went off. She grabbed the mitts and pulled out the French toast bake, setting it on the counter. It needed a few minutes to cool, and then she'd dig in. Her mother wouldn't expect anyone to wait. Not on a morning like today.

"Darrell didn't seem interested in discussing it either. I suppose it's possible that the two of you were so preoccupied that you missed the double moon?" Her father waggled his brows. "When your mother and I were a young couple, we would—"

"Oh my God. Daddy. I just can't with you sometimes." She covered her ears. "I don't want to hear about my parents."

"How do you think you came into this world?" He leaned against the sink, taking his mug from the counter, and lifted it to his lips.

"Not the point." She shook her head, sucking in a deep breath. "How does this happen so fast? In the normal world, it would take a woman a few weeks before she knew. Not a few minutes later."

"This is written in the stars."

"Yeah, well, everything else happening to Darrell and his pack is not." She opened the cupboard, grabbed a plate, and heaved a very large portion of carbs onto her plate. Normally, she wouldn't dare eat like this right before the start of a new ballet.

But what difference did it make now.

"Nope. That's black magic and someone's evil will run amuck."

"It's so unfair and incredibly difficult to handle." She set her plate aside and sucked in a deep breath, letting it out slowly. "One minute I'm the happiest I've ever been. The next I'm dying inside. It's overwhelming, and as soon as I think I've processed it, my mind goes bonkers and my emotions run wild." She swiped her cheeks. "And then Darrell starts in on the doom and gloom and wants to talk about what if he's not here when... when... I can't even say it."

"Come here." Her father held out his strong arms, and she succumbed to the need to be daddy's little girl, even if only for a few precious minutes. He kissed the top of her head as he held her close. "I know this isn't what you wanted right now. But are you going to look me in the eye and tell me that you didn't want your soulmate to be Darrell? That someday you didn't want him to return so you could fall in love, get married, and have a family."

She couldn't lie to her father. Not even if she wanted to. "Well, no."

"Darrell's scared. I suspect he feels as though he failed his father. Is failing as the alpha of his pack." Her father tipped her chin. "And failing you. Add in the fact that right now, he's technically dying and you're pregnant. Well, that's a lot for a young man to take on. He needs you and your strength. But he wants to be your rock. He's an honorable man and feels as though it's his responsibility to take care of you. To protect you. And his family. Him worrying that he might not be here to watch his children grow up is very real for him."

"It's very real for me too, Daddy."

"I know, sweetheart."

She bit back the sob that threatened to roar from deep in her throat. Last night had changed her life forever. She'd given herself completely to Darrell. Nothing could change that, and she didn't want to. "I don't want to let him down, and I want to be there for him, but I can't listen to him talk about it or make provisions for him not being around."

"If today doesn't go well, you might have to." Her father squeezed her biceps.

Footsteps echoed from down the hallway.

"I need to go get changed," her father said, stepping around her. "Eat some breakfast. I'll be back down in about fifteen."

He greeted Darrell with a nod. "Good morning, son."

"Sir," Darrell said.

Her father laughed. "Keep calling me that, and I'll turn you into a toad."

"Then Avery can kiss me, and I'll turn into a prince," Darrell said as he puffed out his chest and smiled with pride.

"That's only if I turn you into a frog," her father said, handing Darrell a covered mug. "I'm guessing that you're a cream and sugar kind of guy."

"What gave me away?" Darrell sipped his coffee, looping his free arm around her waist. Their hips bumped. Being around him sent her heart racing. As comfortable as she was in his arms, this raw energy rattled her nerves, making her a bit self-conscious.

Or maybe it was the smirk on her father's face.

"I just know these things."

"I see." Darrell smiled as if he and her father had some running private joke between them. "When do we leave?"

"Twenty-five minutes." Her father waved his hand. "I've got some news we'll talk about in the car. Gabe is coming with us."

"Where's Trask?" Darrell asked.

"Dealing with some magical recon." Her father waved his hand over his head. "Now eat."

Darrell wasted no time helping himself. "This smells delicious."

"It's fattening too." She snagged her plate and coffee and eased into a chair at the table. She dug her fork into the food and pushed a massive bite into her mouth. The rich flavors melted into her mouth. Her mother loaded so much syrup into the stuff that she didn't need to add more.

But that didn't stop Darrell from doing it. "Well, you do need the extra calories."

She cocked her head and glared.

He lowered his gaze just as her mother waltzed into the room with all the style and grace that made her one of the prettiest ladies in all the world. Avery had always admired her mom and the way she carried herself in any situation.

"Good morning," her mom said. "How's my

baby?" She cupped Avery's chin and kissed her cheek. "Based on the two full moons last night, I'd say you two had a wonderful evening."

"Mother, please," Avery mumbled.

Her mom batted her nose. "Don't *mother* me." She patted Darrell on the shoulder. "Can I get you anything else, son?"

"No. Thank you. And this is absolutely scrumptious, Mrs.—"

"Don't you dare. I'm either Annabell or Mom or even Grandma to you. Whichever you prefer."

Avery groaned. It was never going to stop.

"Yes, ma'am," Darrell said.

Her mother waggled her finger. "Nope. That doesn't work either."

"I'll work on it." Darrell laughed.

"Avery, honey. Where's your phone?" Her mother pulled a mug from the counter and poured a cup of coffee.

"In my pocket, why?" Avery picked at her food.

"Please call your sisters. Especially Amanda. I think she's a little lonely up there in Vermont and is wondering when you and Darrell will move there. Being pregnant and away from her family, even though she has the Fergusons and everyone else there, I'm sure she's looking forward to sharing this experience with her little sister."

Avery shoved her plate aside and dropped her head to the table with a thud.

"Oh, and I thought I'd put two cribs in your suite. Would you two like to pick them out, or should I deal with that myself?" her mother asked.

"I'm not having this conversation now," Avery muttered.

"Okay. I'll do it. No worries." Her mom waved her hand. "I best go help your father."

"Tell me when she's gone, please." Being able to communicate with Darrell through her mind was one good thing that came out of all this. Well, there were others, but until the spell was lifted, she wasn't going to deal with most of it.

"She's gone." Darrell tapped her shoulder. "Look at this." He shoved his phone in her face.

"Oh God. You too?" She stared at an image of a couple of cribs.

"No. My mom." He laughed.

Avery pointed toward the hallway. "I will not be like that with my children."

"Yes, you will. And personally, I love it. We both have great parents." He raked his fingers through his thick shoulder-length hair. "I miss my dad."

She palmed his cheek. "Can I ask you a weird question?"

"Of course."

"How much time will our kids spend as wolves?"

"As babies, more than half their time. It's easier to teach them the ways of being a wolf. Not to mention they will enjoy their wolf form more. They can run and play, versus being helpless in their human form." He leaned forward. "And it will save us—you—money in diapers because they will be housebroken."

She cupped his face, squeezing his cheek. "Don't you ever speak to me like that again. I will not do this alone. It is not me. It will always be us."

"Yes, dear," he said.

"Keep saying that." She released his face. "Because I will always wear the tights in this family."

"Perhaps, but remember, I look damn good in them too."

She cracked a smile. "Yeah, you do."

Her father stuck his head in the kitchen. "All right, you two. Time to roll."

"We just need to do these dishes," she said.

"Your mother will deal with those." He wiggled his index finger. "Time's wasting. Let's go."

She followed her father to the front of the house, her fingers locked with Darrell's, her fairy dust coating his skin like an old sweater. It looked good on him, but he needed his aura to be restored so she could have hers back and her fairy dust didn't have to constantly be put in use.

Her father opened the back door of the family limo. "Gabe, this is Darrell."

Darrell settled into the seat, and she made sure she sat next to him, forcing her father to sit next to his cousin, Gabe.

"Nice to meet you." Darrell extended his hand. "Thanks for helping me and my pack."

"It's unorthodox for you to come with us, but after seeing the double moon last night, I understand why." Gabe was a few years younger than her father, but his position in the coven and on the council put him on equal footing. No one outranked either of them, and they worked together like a well-oiled machine. They almost always agreed on how to deal with anything coven-related, and there hadn't been a time when Gabe hadn't been by her father's side. They were more like brothers in every way.

Not to mention, Gabe was her Wizard Guardian, which was like a godfather. His wife, Jasmine, had been named her Witch Guardian.

"I'd like for that just once not to be the topic of today's discussion," Avery said.

"I'm with her on that," Darrell said as he tried to pull his hand away from her grip, which she'd be damned if she'd allow to happen.

"Well, the good news is that Merlin, the head wizard of the Witches of the Willows, seems to be willing to cooperate." Gabe handed everyone a piece of paper. "But the bad news is that the Wilcox family has disappeared as well as their family's Book of Shadows, which was never registered. According to Merlin, the Wilcoxes come from a line that never practiced."

"That's impossible," her father said. "All blood-lines have black magic. Mine and Trask's are the strongest, but there isn't a family that doesn't have one. Now, I suppose it's possible that it was never passed down to the head of the family."

"But then it should have been reported missing at some point, right?" Avery asked. There was a lot she didn't know about the inner dealings of witch covens and the laws regarding any magic. However, she did know that all black magic was required by law to be registered with the council and if a book, especially a locked book, went missing, and the coven didn't report it, everyone in their clan could be stripped of all their powers. Most wizards wouldn't risk that.

"Merlin is only thirty and took over a few months ago," Gabe said, tapping the paper. "The coven has been in disarray for years without proper leadership."

"Holy shit," Darrell said. "This says that Regan's father, Viner, was the head wizard when we think the spell was cast."

Gabe nodded. "He went missing two weeks later. Since then, they have been through four leaders."

"I've spoken with Merlin, and he's a distant relative of Viner's, and the reason they have had such a large turnover is partly due to three deaths," her father said.

"What did they die of?" Darrell asked, leaning forward.

Avery held her breath, waiting for the blow that she knew deep in the pit of her stomach was coming.

"They don't know, but the symptoms present

like early aging," her father admitted. "Many want to leave the coven."

"So they know something is hinky," Avery said under her breath, staring out the window as the limo turned off the highway and onto a busy road not far from Orange County where most of the Witches of the Willows coven was located.

Being a royal meant her life decisions had to be above reproach. Everything she did was under the microscope of her coven council, but also the governing council, the one that Gabe and her father headed. She couldn't get a tattoo, even an approved one, without everyone needing to know.

"But they never reported anything," she whispered.

"Actually, that's not true. When Merlin took over ten days ago, he contacted the council," Gabe said. "And requested a formal inquisition. It's the only reason why we know so much now."

"So, why will we meet with him if he doesn't know where the book is or where the Wilcox family disappeared to?" Darrell asked what she had been thinking.

"Because he's been working on a spell that will snap their Book of Shadows back to where it was locked. Trask gave him the necessary tools. That's what he was doing this morning. If Merlin can do that, we can trace where it came from and, hopefully, unlock the spells and find a reversal," her father said.

"We can work with this," she whispered, knowing it was a long shot, but it was better than no shot.

"We're searching for a needle in a haystack," Darrell muttered. "We need to find the source. The exact spell. I don't need to be a witch to know without that, my pack, you, and me are toast."

"I know you're frustrated, son," her father said, leaning forward. "But we bought ourselves three days. Before tossing in the towel or thinking the worst, we need to start with what we know and can use. The Witches of the Willows are willing to work with us without Gabe and me forcing them. This is good because we can trust their magic."

"Are you sure about that?" Darrell asked behind tight lips. "Because they seem pretty damn unstable to me."

"No," her father said, reaching out, resting his hand on her knee, knowing she needed a douse of his strength. "Merlin is leading them in a positive direction. I had the pleasure of teaching him a few years ago, and he's a good wizard with good intentions. And Trask was with him last night and into the early hours of this morning."

"Where is Trask now?" Darrell asked.

"He's needed elsewhere," her father said. "But he's watching. We know what we're doing."

"Trust my dad," she whispered with her chin on Darrell's shoulder.

Darrell turned his head and met her gaze. "I trust your father absolutely. But anyone related to the witch who did this to us, not only do I distrust, but I want the curse to stick with them when we're wiped clean of it."

10

"*I* know you want me to stay with Avery, but I think I should be in on this conversation." Darrell glanced over his shoulder, looking toward Avery where she leaned against the limo with her arms folded, glaring at him and her father. "This isn't just about me and Avery. Our babies. But my entire pack. My entire family."

"What do you think you can add to this meeting?" Albert asked.

"What's he saying?" Avery projected.

"A different perspective and let's not forget, I was there when the spell was cast," Darrell said.

"That is if Regan Wilcox is indeed the one who cast the spell."

"We both know this is the only logical explanation." Darrell didn't like arguing with a man he respected and the father of the woman he loved, but no way would he sit idly behind and do nothing. "I might be able to pick up something or add a memory I'd forgotten that can help us find the Wilcox family, the book, and make sure no one else dies." He arched a brow. "I also have a heightened sense of smell. I get you are a powerful wizard, but you'd have to do magic to do what I can do by breathing."

"Don't ignore me," Avery said.

"I'm not. But this isn't very easy and I can't have a conversation with your dad while I'm fielding questions from you. Give me a break, please?"

"I don't want my daughter left alone, and I need Gabe at my side. Which means I'm relying on you to take care of my little girl if something goes sideways in there."

"If this works, I'll be taking care of her and our children for a long time. She needs to come with us. She was there that day, too."

"No," her father said, shaking his head. "She's already at risk. Why put her in the line of potentially greater danger?"

"You told me yesterday that it was best not to have a wall between us. What's changed?"

"Nothing. I lied yesterday." Albert let out a long breath, resting his hands on his hips. "Besides wanting you and Avery to have time together, I feared you might shift into a wolf and run off. Shifting could destroy her aura."

Darrell swallowed his pride. He probably would have lied too. "I can feel her aura now, and she's worried and angry, which only weakens both of us. I'm sorry, sir, but she needs to go where I go, and I'm going to meet with Merlin."

Albert pinched the bridge of his nose. "You're right. You're right," he whispered, nodding his head. "Locking her up in the limo isn't going to protect her, much less save either one of you."

He placed a hand on the prince's shoulder. "I will lay down my life if it means she'll be fine."

"I know you would, son. But understand, she'd do the same for you and excuse me for being a selfish prick, but I'd rather she didn't. Not to mention, she can't. She holds the future in her belly. All my daughters will. That's a lot for this old man to bear." He sighed. "You're not a witch. You're not one of these people's kind, and they won't like a wolf hanging around while I probe into their lives, so please, follow my lead, okay?"

"I can do that, sir."

"Seriously, stop the sir shit. You're family. Call me Albert."

"Albert," Darrell said with a thick lump lodged in his throat. "Let's get this party started." Darrell waved Avery over, and she wasted no time racing to his side.

He looped his arm over her shoulders, kissing her cheek, lingering a little longer than he should have. "We're all meeting with Merlin," he whispered in her ear. "Stay close to me, okay?"

"I won't leave your side," she said with her hand resting on his hip as they followed her father and Gabe down a long, windy path lined with green bushes and colorful flowers, including red and white roses and purple and yellow tulips.

The brick building in front of them stood tall, reaching its three stories into the blue sky like fingers. A sign that read Witches of the Willows School of Magic hung over a wooden double door with brass handles. Albert slammed his knuckles on the wood, knocking three times, and stepped back.

They all waited as seconds ticked by like sand in an hourglass.

The big doors swung open and a tall, skinny man appeared. "Welcome, I'm Merlin. It's a pleasure to see you again, Prince Albert." Merlin extended his hand, his long fingers showing signs of arthritis. "I wish it were under different circumstances."

"Us as well." Prince Albert nodded.

"As you can see by my appearance"—Merlin waved a hand over his wrinkled face—"we don't have much time. I have aged another few years overnight. There is not one wizard in my coven that will step up after me. Many are running to seek shelter with others."

"That won't save them," Albert said.

"The curse is already in everyone's blood," Gabe added as they walked through a long corridor.

Empty classrooms lined each side. Pictures of witches in classrooms performing various spells lined the walls.

"I have tried to explain this, but my people are scared. Many years ago, we suffered our first death from this curse, but we didn't know why, and it didn't happen again until a month ago. Since then, it's been a rapid decline. On my council, there are only three of us left. They are waiting in one of the craft labs."

"How sick are they?" Darrell asked. When he'd spoken to his mother, a few wolves were complaining of increased pain, but it seemed things weren't progressing as rapidly as with the wizards.

"I've been able to create a potion that slows the process down, but we're almost out, and it doesn't appear to be as effective anymore."

"How is the spell coming to locate the Book of Shadows?" Gabe asked.

"It's complete, but it will kill me if I use it." Merlin turned a corner, and they looped up a flight of stairs.

The building should have been filled with the sounds of witches learning their craft. Instead, a deafening silence filled the empty space.

"Trask believes if I surrender my powers to one of you and have you cast the spell, it would work." Merlin stopped in front of a classroom.

"But that would transfer the black magic," Avery said with wide eyes.

"It would, but Trask also thinks if we give my powers to an infected, it won't be as powerful," Merlin said as he stepped into the lab.

"I've already been able to pull part of the spell out from my daughter and Darrell." Albert scratched the back of his head. "The governing council is doing their best with the sample I gave them, but they don't have a mark yet."

"They might not find it since the book is locked." Merlin nodded to two men standing in front of a table filled with burners, small cauldrons, and other things necessary for mixing potions.

The men nodded back but kept working.

"I can use the same spell to pull some of it out if we decide putting the powers in Avery is the only hope," Albert said.

"What!" Darrell snapped his head in the direction of Albert. "No fucking way. I won't allow you to put my mate at risk like that. It could kill her. And our babies."

Avery gripped his hand, her pulse pounding against his skin.

"She might be *your* mate, but she's *my* daughter, and as you said out there a few minutes ago, you both die if we do nothing."

"Cast the powers into me," Darrell said with a low growl. "I know it can be done. You did with Jackson."

"That was different," Albert said, inching closer, anger firing from his gray eyes. "I had to make him an untouchable to keep my sister from killing him. I can't make you an untouchable with that spell inside you."

Avery squeezed his biceps. "And if we cast

191

wizard powers in you without an outside aura and an inside aura disappearing, it will suck the life energy out of you in minutes. Killing us both." She took his hand and placed it on her stomach. "And our children. Casting it into me is our only option."

Darrell yanked his arm free, taking a few steps back and raking a hand through his unruly hair. "There has to be another way."

"That's what we're looking for, but our time is running out," Albert said, staring at Darrell. "I don't want to do this any more than you do, but these wizards are dying off faster than your pack is getting sick, and when they are all gone, your pack will die off fast, taking my daughter and grandchildren with you." He pointed toward the ceiling. "We don't know what kind of ripple effect that will have on Amanda and Jackson. Or Arianna, Alicia, and their future mates."

"And we don't know if the spell will then start in the royal family," Merlin said. "If they die off, we'll have mayhem."

Darrell turned his back, folding his arms across his chest. His gut tightened, and the room blurred. He blinked five times, trying to snap everything into focus.

Avery's soft, loving hands glided up his shoulder

blades. "It's the only way," she whispered, her lips kissing the side of his neck. "I might not be the most powerful witch, but I can do this."

Darrell took a deep, calming breath. "What happens if this works and it snaps the Book of Shadows back? What then?"

"I unlock the black magic, and then we can make this right," Albert said, placing a firm hand on Darrell's shoulder. "All I need is that book."

"What about the Wilcox family? Will they be brought to justice?" Darrell asked.

"If they survive, they will be stripped of their powers," Albert said with a tight voice. "And locked away."

Darrell turned, locking gazes with Albert. "And if this doesn't work?"

Albert said nothing, but he didn't have to.

"We need to do this," Avery said, palming his cheek, forcing him to look her in the eye. "For your pack... for us. For our future and for what's coming."

Darrell squeezed his eyes closed. He could be the macho alpha and pull rank with his mate, or he could do the right thing for everyone concerned.

"What do you need me to do?" Darrell pulled Avery to his chest, holding on to her for dear life.

"You'll have to fight the urge to let go of her aura no matter what happens," Albert said. "You give it all back, you die, making all this pointless."

"I don't plan on meeting my maker for a long time, so let's get this freak show on the road."

11

While Avery practiced witchcraft every day, her higher-level skills were rusty. All witches had to go through courses that would prepare them for the use of black magic, but since her fifteenth birthday, she hadn't actually performed any of the illegal spells permitted during training, only legal ones.

And she'd never had to absorb someone else's powers. After seeing what it did to her father to give them up to Jackson, even momentarily, she couldn't believe she was agreeing to it.

Life or death.

She chose life.

"You're going to be entering what we call the

empty space," Merlin said. "The potion will allow you to see the keeper of the locked books."

"Why can't we just call upon this keeper to give it back?" Darrell said, not hiding his frustration or his sarcasm.

"Only the head wizard of any coven can get it back, and they risk not being able to make it back," Merlin said, his damn even tone making her want to crawl out of her skin.

"This is sounding like a dumber plan by the second," Darrell muttered.

"Just remember to trust your instincts," her father said, holding her shoulders.

Right, because being a ballerina had prepared her for this.

"He will point you to where the book is, but he can't go with you," Merlin said. "And don't let him distract you."

She nodded. "Anything else?"

"Get the book, hold it tight, and cast the spell to bring you and the book back," Merlin said, clasping his hands together.

"Are you ready?" her father asked, leaning against the table, his arms folded.

Darrell stood next to him, same position, with a deep scowl on his face.

She smoothed down her jeans and took in a deep breath. Taking even a weakened wizard's power would be difficult. No matter how much she prepared herself for the collision between her powers and his, she could not predict how her body would react.

Much less Darrell's, and since they were connected through her aura, he would most likely feel and see everything she did.

"Ready as I'll ever be," she said.

"Drink this." Merlin handed her a small test tube filled with a smoky purple liquid. "It will help protect your connection to Darrell. And whatever you do, don't project to each other."

Her father glanced at Darrell as he placed a fatherly hand on his shoulder. "Go sit next to her. That might help too."

Darrell nodded as he walked slowly, his feet scuffing the dulled tile floor. He sat on the hard wooden chair next to her, holding her hand, his thumb gently rubbing her skin.

"While I cast the spell, Prince Albert will try to contain the spell Regan hexed," Merlin spoke in a monotone voice. "From the time my powers leave my body, we will have only a few minutes to snap the book back and cast the powers back to me."

"How many minutes, exactly?" Avery asked.

"Maybe five," her father answered.

"Here we go," Merlin said. "The witch and this wizard are one. We are bonded together until the deed is done. Out of the cauldron and into wait, I cast the powers of fate."

She gritted her teeth as a fire burned deep in the pit of her gut.

Darrell growled low, squeezing her hand, turning her knuckles white.

"I shall regain my strength in my sister form to pull back the book that fell into warn."

As Merlin spoke, her body shivered as her pores opened up, allowing a gray cloud of smoke to settle into her bloodstream. A surge of energy, like the crackle of a lightning bolt, exploded from her toes to her head. Her aura shifted, pulling closer to her body. She shoved it away, mentally reaching out to Darrell, trying not to project.

"The magic rises in the west, setting where we need it best," Merlin said. "Out of the cauldron and into the past, find the Witches of the Willows Book of Shadows from the tree of the last."

"Now," her father commanded as he held a ball of white smoke between his hands, his body wrinkling like skin soaked in water for hours.

She closed her eyes, ignoring the sharp, stabbing pain in her temples as she stepped into the past, following the trail of fireflies leading the way. Visions of people she'd never met floated by.

"Hurry," her father said in a voice so soft, she barely heard him.

"This way," a man said, standing near a willow tree.

"Who are you?" she asked, following him down a path that led to a small cabin. She had to be sure this wasn't some trick in this weird place that didn't really exist.

"I'm the keeper of secrets," he said with an eerie smile. "I have what you seek."

"Where?"

"Why don't you visit with me for a while. It gets lonely in the dark world."

"I can't. Wizards and werewolves are dying." She wanted to add she was too, but she wasn't sure that would help.

"We can take a walk by the pond. It's so pretty there. It's right on the way," the man said.

"I need to get to the book," she said, taking a few steps forward, but she had no idea if the cabin in front of her was the cabin.

"I know," the man said with a long sigh. "I can tell you have resolve for your quest." He waved his finger at the building, which seemed to move closer and closer. "Be sure

you get the right one, or more unthinkable things will happen."

She took off running until she stood at the door. She could no longer hear her father.

Or feel Darrell.

That had to be bad.

Pushing back the front door, she entered the cabin, shocked by the number of Shadow books on the shelves. She scanned them, going from left to right, top to bottom. Tears welled in her eyes as she came to the last shelf, but she still hadn't found the one she needed.

She was about to start scanning again, when she noticed a desk in the corner with an old, dusty book sitting on top, the Witches of the Willows crest embedded on its leather case. When she took the book in her hands, her skin prickled with fire.

"Out of the cauldron, out of the empty space, cast this mix of wizard and witch back to the right place. Keep this book safe through the passage of time and ease the locks that bind the rhyme."

Her body shook as the cabin she stood in crumbled to the ground. The man she'd seen waved to her, but she ignored him, looking for the safe passage from this nonexistent plane. Merlin said she would know it when she saw it. Turning in a full circle, she could see the school to the east. Running as fast as she could, she approached the front door. She raced through the corridors, clutching the book tight until she found the room that housed her body.

And the man she loved.

She busted through the door but stopped dead in her tracks when she saw Darrell sprawled out on the floor, foaming at the mouth.

No!

She raced to her body.

"Out of the cauldron and into the witch's meme. Reverse the spell and return the witch to her frame. Bring the Book of Shadows to the wizard of logic, giving him permission to seek the one who can break the cursed magic."

The room spun around her as if she were the sun and the lab the earth. Her stomach twisted and knotted. Flames coated her skin as she snapped into her body.

"Avery," her father said.

But she couldn't answer. Nor could she see anything but blurred images. She blinked a few times, but nothing helped.

She licked her dry, cracked lips and tried to speak again. "Darrell," she croaked out.

"He's very weak." Her father gave her a kiss on the cheek before helping her to the ground. "Lie next to him. Hold him. Let your fairy dust fly. It will help."

"Dad, did I do it?" She rested her head and

hand on Darrell's chest. His breathing was shallow and his heart beat so slow she could barely feel it.

"You did," he said. "Now, I need you to rest so I can do my part. Can you do that, my little girl? Can you let yourself sleep?"

"Will it help Darrell?"

"Yes," her father said.

She let her breathing fall in line with Darrell's and pushed as much of her fairy dust as she could over him, knowing that it was his inner aura that was killing him, and there was nothing she could do about that.

Her mind wandered back to when she'd been five years old.

"Avery, are you ready?" Miss Tammy asked.

"Yes." Avery jumped up from her seat and bounced to the center of the room.

Darrell took her hand and smiled.

The music began and he effortlessly led her through the routine. In his arms, it was as if she belonged there.

Glancing in the mirror, she gasped at the reflection of her and Darrell as adults, not children…

"I love you, Darrell," she said.

"I love you, too."

12

"Daddy, do something." Avery held Darrell's head in her lap. His breaths were still shallow, and his heart rate reached a dangerously slow pace.

"I need to unlock the book first," he said from across the room.

Merlin and his two men lay on the floor, near death, not far from where she cradled her mate in her arms.

"He's fading fast," she whispered, pressing her lips on his cold, clammy forehead. "What went wrong?"

"Nothing," her father said as he poured some liquid into a beaker.

"He didn't break our bond?"

"No, but his resolve to protect what is his is so strong that he let you have all but the thinnest layer of your life aura."

"How could he do that without being a witch?" She glanced in her father's direction, who looked up from his potion for only a brief second. "Oh, Daddy, you didn't?"

"I did what I thought was best for everyone," her father said with a dark tone. "And he begged me to make sure you had what was needed to complete the task. That you and his children would be safe. Bigger picture, little girl."

"I could have done it without you casting a—"

"He was starting to tap into your inner aura, and it ended up taking you twelve minutes," her father said as he poured some liquid into a tiny cup. "If I hadn't made it so he could let go of some, you'd both be dead."

"But now he's dying in my arms," she said, holding back the tears. Darrell didn't need her crying. He needed her to be strong.

Her father handed her the cup. "Give this to him. It will help while I unlock the book, which will take a little while."

"He doesn't have much time." She parted

Darrell's lips, letting the potion trickle into his mouth and throat. He didn't move. Didn't cough.

Nothing.

"They are dying too," she said, pointing to Merlin and his fellow wizards.

"I gave them the same potion before you snapped back. Now hush, child, and let me work."

She ran her fingers through Darrell's thick, dark hair, feeling every strand glide across her skin. She'd never been in love and in less than a week, she'd fallen head over heels.

Soulmates.

Fated mates.

The Legend of the Fated Moons.

Parents. She was going to be a mother. A fate she could no longer deny if she tried. She could feel her children growing inside her womb. It was as if they were giving her strength and energy to fight for their father.

Deep down she knew Darrell would be the only man she'd ever love, but now she might not get the chance to really give him everything he deserved.

And she'd never get the chance to dance with him, much less choreograph a piece only their love could conjure.

"Stay with me," she whispered.

Nothing.

The sound of lightning crackled as her father poured a potion over the book. "Out of the cauldron, I unlock the black magic by the Witches of the Willows, which is protected in this book. Take the spells and let them look. The pages filling left and right, open this case and find the spite. Out of the cauldron and into light, guide this wizard to the sight."

The room filled with a pitch-black smoke, making it impossible to see.

"I'm in," her father said. "And there is a reversing spell."

Tears streamed down her cheeks as a guttural sob escaped the pit of her stomach. "Please, Daddy, hurry."

In seconds, her father was at her side. "Out of the cauldron and into the hollows of a cave, take this death spell, cast it out to sea and heal the brave. Heal the soul that burned with black, taking the spell back. Put out the fire and fill with ice, giving this wolf, his kind, his mate, and all the other tormented by hell, might." Her father splashed something over Darrell, and his body shook and his skin turned white.

"I don't think it's working," she whispered as

Darrell's body temperature dropped drastically. She could see his breath like he was out in the freezing elements of the Great North.

"It's working." Her father sat down beside her, putting a tender hand over her shoulder. "He's pushing out the spell with every exhale."

"He's so cold. Werewolves aren't supposed to be cold."

"I'll get him a blanket, but trust me, my little precious one, your soulmate will be fine."

She held him tight, kissing his cold skin. "I love you," she whispered.

Darrell gritted his teeth, doing all he could to hang on to the tiny piece of Avery that the spell cast by her father allowed. He should sacrifice himself to protect her and his children. They deserved to live more than he did. His pack would have another leader and if she was successful, then she'd be able to save both the Witches of the Willows and his pack.

But he promised her father he'd fight for their union and that was the only way Albert would agree to cast the spell.

His vision blurred, and the room faded to black.

His body dropped to the floor, even though he tried to keep himself upright.

Scorching pain ripped through his veins. He could only hope that he was helping Avery.

Not hurting her.

He shivered as a cold wave flowed through his bloodstream. His heart slowed, and he could no longer hear anything. He tried opening his mouth, but he couldn't move.

Panic gripped his heart.

Then the world went dark.

Damp.

Nothing.

"Darrell?" Avery's voice echoed in his mind. It sounded like the purest music he'd ever heard. "Can you hear me?"

He blinked his eyes, but nothing snapped into focus. Everything around him was one big gray blur.

"He needs more rest," a man's voice boomed. "Let him sleep."

"It's been two days," Avery said.

Darrell cleared his throat, licking his dry, cracked lips. "Two days?" he asked in the faintest of whispers.

"You've been out in a deep sleep for that long."

Warm lips touched his cheek, and he let out a moan, enjoying the tender touch of his mate.

"What happened?" He tried to focus on the body he knew lay next to him on the... a soft bed? Sofa? Where the hell was he? He blinked a few times, squeezing his eyes tight, but still, he couldn't make out anything. "Where am I?"

"The Ferguson farm. In Vermont," a familiar female voice said. "Trask and my father thought it was the safest place. Unfortunately, the paranormal and human worlds are all abuzz about the second pairing of the Fated Moons and some creatures are scared of what might be coming."

"Our children will be good, not evil," he managed. "Was the spell reversed?"

"Yes," the male voice said.

Darrell knew that had to be Albert, meaning he wasn't dead.

That was good news.

"Avery?"

"I'm right here," she said, her hand rubbing up and down his bare chest.

Bed.

With Avery.

Half-naked? With her father in the room.

That's embarrassing.

He rubbed his eyes before trying to shift to a sitting position.

"You shouldn't be moving," Albert said.

Darrell didn't listen as he pushed a pillow behind his head, pulling the covers halfway up his body. A wave of nausea hit his stomach. He swallowed as colors and shapes formed.

Albert sat on the foot of the bed and Avery next to him.

"I feel like I got hit by a truck," Darrell managed, taking the glass of water Avery offered. "I take it Avery succeeded?"

"I did," she said, smiling. "No one in your pack has any more symptoms. Merlin is doing well, and his coven is slowly returning to normal."

"And what about Regan and her family?" Darrell asked. He didn't wish the worst for them, but he certainly wanted justice.

"The family was able to keep Regan alive until a few weeks before your father died, which sent the spell into action. My father said right before Regan passed, they harvested parts of the spell and cast them into her sister."

"That's fucked up. What kind of parent would do that to their kid?" Darrell asked.

"They thought if they could keep their family from dying from the adverse effects of using blocked black magic, it would give them time to find an antidote without coming to me," Albert said.

"The rest of the family has been taken into custody," Avery said.

"I need to call my mom."

"She's downstairs with mine—"

"My mother is here?" he interrupted Avery, trying to hide his mortification. God only knows what his mother might have told his mate.

Or her family.

Or the Fergusons.

"We had to call her, son." Alfred stood. "I'll go let her know you're awake."

"Sir?"

"I'm going to break you of that horrible habit," Alfred said. "What is it?"

"Can you take your time telling my mom I've woken from the dead. I'd like a few—"

Alfred held up his hand. "Say no more. But I won't be able to keep her at bay too long, and I feel I should warn you that your mom, my wife, and Avery's sisters have already planned out the wedding and the baby shower. They assumed you'd be awake in a few days. It's taking place in two weeks."

"I haven't even proposed. Or bought a ring," he said with a slight chuckle, though it hurt to laugh.

"We have heirloom rings for that and you knocked up my daughter. I think official proposals are out the window."

"Daddy. That was rude," Avery said, but with a smile.

If a heart could grin, then Darrell's filled his chest.

"I'll be back, and I'm bringing the doctor, just to be safe." Albert slipped from the room.

Darrell let his eyes adjust slightly as he soaked in Avery's beauty. "Thank you."

"For what?"

"Saving my sorry ass."

"You're welcome." She rested her head on his chest. "Because, you know, I wear the tights in this family."

Even though it strained his muscles, he wrapped his arms around her body. "Yes, dear."

"Oh, a woman could get used to hearing that." She laughed. "I resigned as principal while you were sleeping."

"It was for the best, considering everything." He

kissed her temple. "But I will miss telling you what to do onstage because something tells me that's the only place I would have held any power in this relationship."

"You're right about that," she said, glancing up at him with a glimmer of mischief in her eyes. "I know our future is a little on hold because of this whole Legend of the Fated Moons, but when it's all over, I do want very much to choreograph with you."

"We will." He sighed. His eyes grew heavy. "I'm sorry. I'm so tired." He rested his head against hers. "I promise to love you forever."

"I will love you right back."

13

TWO WEEKS LATER...

*D*arrell sat at the makeshift bar in the barn at the Ferguson farm in Vermont and stared at his bride. The last two weeks had passed in a haze. He'd spent six days in bed, recovering from having black magic cast from his body.

Boy, had that been an experience. One he hoped he never had to repeat.

A couple little wolfairy pups raced between his legs, pausing to tug at his slacks. He chuckled, bending over to pat them on the head. "Who do we have here?" He knelt down. Little Jasper, one of Nico and Isadore's kids, jumped on his lap and licked his face. "Aren't you cute." He wiggled. Darrell set the wolfairy back down and the rest of them raced off as he glanced back at his beautiful bride.

Avery hugged her sister Amanda and then smoothed down the front of her wedding dress. A simple strapless gown that made her look like the royal princess she was. She glided across the room, waving and smiling at everyone she passed. How the hell had he gotten so lucky?

"You can stop gawking now, son. She married you," Albert said as he handed Darrell a glass of red wine.

"I like gawking." Darrell raised his glass in a toast. "Besides, I catch you staring at your wife all the time."

"I know." Albert laughed. "To soulmates. Fated mates. Or whatever a given species calls them."

Darrell clinked his glass and then took a long swig, enjoying the rich cabernet flowing down his throat in a slow burn. "I want you to know that I will always do my best to protect her."

"I know you will," Albert said. "You're a good man."

"I can only hope I'm half the man you are and my father was."

"Just be your own man and take good care of my little girl."

"You can count on me for that." While Darrell missed his father dearly, Albert would make the finest father-in-law a man could ask for.

"Now all I have to do is sit around and wait for two more wolves who somehow managed to imprint on my other girls," Albert said as Avery stepped closer. "And more double moons will appear in the sky." He laughed.

"Two of my favorite men." Avery looped her arm over Darrell's shoulders, leaning her hip against the barstool.

"You have more?" Darrell asked.

"Um, well, yeah. Like every little male wolfairy that's running around this place." She waved her hand over her chest. "I understand now what you and your mother meant by them being almost cuter in their wolf form. I'm getting used to the idea of dealing with puppies."

Darrell laughed, kissing her shoulder.

"I know it's not ideal for all of you to be living here and we'll miss you," Albert said.

"Dad, you can come visit anytime you want. Chaz and his family have made that perfectly clear."

"I know." He kissed Avery's temple. "While it's possible we're being overly cautious since nothing like what happened when Chaz first met Daphne has been going on with this legend, there is still a lot of fear in the witch world about witchcraft and fairy magic mixing."

"It's so ridiculous." Darrell pointed toward Trask and Hollie.

Trask held his little girl, Ali, who was in her human form while she played with her fairy dust, showing off some of her own special brand of magic. She was a unique creature being a wolfairy witch. She didn't need to command the elements and spells the same way witches did. And her fairy magic was purer than even Daphne's, one of the strongest royal fairies out there.

"They aren't evil," Avery said.

"But there are evil creatures who would like to harness their magic," Alfred said. "Until the final pairing, and all my grandbabies are born, it's safer for you to be here. Besides, as you're learning, your fairy magic needs refinement." He tapped Avery's nose. "Now, if you will excuse me, I'm going to go find my wife and take her for a spin around the dance floor."

Avery glanced up at Darrell and smiled. "Thank you."

"For what?"

"Letting them do all this when I know you would have preferred to forgo ceremony."

He shrugged. "It's one day out of the rest of our lives." He loosened his tie. "Although, I do hate these monkey suits."

"Want to sneak out of here and into your birthday suit?" She waggled her brows.

"You don't have to ask this wolf that question twice." He grabbed her hand and tugged. "But we better hurry before someone stops us and starts asking us about names again."

"My sister wants to stick with tradition and go with Aubry and Austin."

"What about you? What do you want?"

She paused at the door, palming his cheek. "The girl's name, you get to pick. But I'm going to demand the boy be named after your father. We can use Albert as a middle name. That's close enough to tradition. But I won't change my mind on this."

"It's settled, then. Brandon Albert. It's a good name." He smiled. "Our daughter will be Twilight Echo. Totally breaking tradition."

She cocked her head. "Why that name?"

"Because it was the musical piece we danced to when I imprinted on you."

ABOUT THE AUTHOR

Jen Talty is the *USA Today* Bestselling Author of Contemporary Romance, Romantic Suspense, and Paranormal Romance. In the fall of 2020, her short story was selected and featured in a 1001 Dark Nights Anthology.

Regardless of the genre, her goal is to take you on a ride that will leave you floating under the sun with warmth in your heart. She writes stories about broken heroes and heroines who aren't necessarily looking for romance, but in the end, they find the kind of love books are written about :).

She first started writing while carting her kids to one hockey rink after the other, averaging 170 games per year between 3 kids in 2 countries and 5 states. Her first book, IN TWO WEEKS was originally published in 2007. In 2010 she helped form a publishing company (Cool Gus Publishing) with *NY*

Times Bestselling Author Bob Mayer where she ran the technical side of the business through 2016.

Jen is currently enjoying the next phase of her life…the empty nester! She and her husband reside in Jupiter, Florida.

Grab a glass of vino, kick back, relax, and let the romance roll in…

Sign up for my Newsletter (https://dl.bookfunnel.com/82gm8b9k4y) where I often give away free books before publication.

Join my private Facebook group (https://www.facebook.com/groups/191706547909047/) where I post exclusive excerpts and discuss all things murder and love!

Never miss a new release. Follow me on Amazon:amazon.com/author/jentalty

And on Bookbub: bookbub.com/authors/jen-talty

ALSO BY JEN TALTY

Brand new series: SAFE HARBOR!

Mine To Keep

Mine To Save

Mine To Protect

Mine to Hold

Mine to Love

Check out LOVE IN THE ADIRONDACKS!

Shattered Dreams

An Inconvenient Flame

The Wedding Driver

Clear Blue Sky

Blue Moon

Before the Storm

NY STATE TROOPER SERIES (also set in the Adirondacks!)

In Two Weeks

Dark Water

Deadly Secrets